"Kate will make you a wonderful wife."

Rorie spoke forcefully, feeling both disillusioned and indignant. But she refused to let him know how much he'd hurt her.

Clay drew a hand across his eyes; she could feel his exhaustion from the other side of the room. "The last thing in the world I want to do is hurt Kate."

"Then don't."

He stared at her and Rorie tried to send him a smile.

"I don't know what's best anymore," Clay admitted quietly.

"I do," Rorie said with unwavering confidence. "Think about it, Clay. We were alone together for hours—we shared something beautiful with Star Bright and her foal. And we shared a few stolen kisses in the moonlight. That's all."

There was a long silence between them, and when Clay finally spoke, his voice sounded hoarse. "So it was just the moonlight?"

"Of course," she lied. "What else could it have been?"

Debbie Macomber is an American writer born in the state of Washington, where she still lives. She and her electrician husband have four children, all of them teenagers. They also support a menagerie that includes horses, cats, a dog and some guinea pigs. Debbie's successful writing career actually started in childhood, when her brother copied—and sold—her diary! She's gone on to a considerably wider readership since then, as a prolific and popular author published in several different romance lines. She says she wrote her first book because she fell in love with Harlequin Romances—and wanted to write her own.

Books by Debbie Macomber

A Little
Bit Country

Debbie Macomber

Harlequin Books

TORONTO • NEW YORK • LONDON
AMSTERDAM • PARIS • SYDNEY • HAMBURG
STOCKHOLM • ATHENS • TOKYO • MILAN

ISBN 0-373-03038-X

Harlequin Romance first edition March 1990

CHAPTER ONE

"HELP! FIRE!" Rorie Campbell cried as she leapt out of the small foreign car. Smoke billowed from beneath the hood, rising like a burnt offering to a disgruntled god. Rorie raced across the road, and a black-and-white cow moseyed through the pasture toward her, stopping at the split-rail fence. Soulful brown eyes studied her, as if the cow were wondering what all the commotion was about.

"It's not even my car," Rorie told the sympathetic heifer, pointing in the direction of the vehicle. "All of a sudden smoke started coming out."

The cow regarded her blankly, chewing its cud, then returned lazily to the shade of a huge oak tree.

"I think it's on fire. Dan's going to kill me for this," Rorie finished lamely as she watched the disinterested animal saunter away. "Oh, heavens, I don't know what to do." There was no water in sight and even if there had been, Rorie didn't have any way of hauling it to the car. She was so desperate that she was talking to cattle—and she'd almost expected the creature to advise her.

"Howdy."

Rorie whirled around to discover a man astride a chestnut stallion. Silhouetted against the warm afternoon sun, he looked like an apparition smiling down at her from the side of the hill opposite Dan's car.

"Hello." Rorie's faith in a benign destiny increased tenfold in that moment. "Boy, am I glad to see another human being." She'd been on this road for the past two hours and hadn't encountered another car in either direction.

"What seems to be the problem?" Leather creaked as the man swung out of the saddle with an ease that bespoke years of experience.

"I...I don't know," Rorie said, flapping her hands in frustration. "Everything was going along just great when all of a sudden the car started smoking like crazy."

"That's steam."

"Steam! You mean the car isn't on fire?"

The man flipped the reins over his horse's head to dangle to the ground and walked over to the hood of the sports car. It was then that Rorie realized the man wasn't a man at all, but a boy. Sixteen, possibly older, but not by much. Not that Rorie was particular. She was just grateful someone had stopped. "A friend of mine insisted I drive his MGB up to Seattle. I knew I shouldn't, deep down inside. I should have known that if anything went wrong, I'd be at a total loss over what to do. I should have known..."

The youth whipped a large blue-starred hankie from the hip pocket of his faded jeans and used it to protect his hand while he raised the hood of her car. The instant he did, a great white cloud of steam swirled up like mist from a graveyard in a horror movie.

"I...thought I'd take the scenic route," Rorie explained, frantically waving her hand in front of her face to dispel the vapor. "The man at the gas station a hundred miles back said this is beautiful country. He said I'd miss some of the best scenery in Oregon if I stuck to the freeway." Rorie realized she was chattering, but she'd never experienced this type of situation before nor felt quite so helpless.

"It's not only the best scenery in the state, it tops the whole country, if you ask me," the youth murmured absently while he carefully checked several thick black hoses beneath the raised hood.

Rorie looked at her watch and moaned. If she wasn't in Seattle before six, she was going to lose her hotel reservation. This vacation wasn't starting out well—not at all. And she'd had such high expectations for the next two weeks.

"It looks like you've got a leak in your water pump," the teenager stated, sounding as though he knew what he was talking about. "But it's hard to tell with all that fancy stuff they got in these foreign cars. Clay can tell you for sure."

"Clay?"

"My brother."

"Is he a mechanic?" Rorie's hopes soared.

"He's done his share of working on cars, but he's not a mechanic."

Rorie gnawed on her lower lip as her spirits plummeted again. Her first concern was getting to a phone. She'd make the necessary arrangements to get the car repaired and then call the hotel to ask if they'd hold her room. Depending on how close she was to the nearest town, Rorie figured it would take at least an hour for a tow truck to get to her and then another for it to get her car to a garage. Once there, the repairs shouldn't require too much time. Just how much trouble could fixing a water pump be?

"How far is it to the phone?"

The youth grinned and pointed toward his horse. "Just over that ridge..."

Rorie relaxed. At least that part wasn't going to be much of a problem.

"...about ten miles," the teenager finished.

"Ten miles?" Rorie leaned her weight against the side of the car and let the frustration work its way through her weary bones. She swore this was the last time she'd ever take the scenic route and the last time she'd ever let Dan talk her into borrowing his car!

"Don't worry, you won't have to walk. Venture can handle both of us. You don't appear to weigh much."

"Venture?" Rorie was beginning to feel like an echo.

"My horse."

Rorie's gaze zoomed to the stallion, who had lowered his head to sample the tall sweet hillside grass. Now that she had a chance to study him, she realized what an extraordinarily large animal he was. Rorie hadn't been on the back of a horse since she was a child. Somehow, the experience of riding a pony in a slow circle with a bunch of other six year-olds all those years ago didn't lend her much confidence now.

"You...you want me to ride double with you?" She was wearing a summer dress and mounting a horse might prove rather...interesting. She eyed the stallion, wondering how she could manage to climb into the saddle and still maintain her dignity.

"You wearing a dress and all could make that difficult." The boy rubbed the side of his jaw, looking doubtful.

"I could wait here until someone else comes along," she offered.

The teenager used his index finger to set his snapbrim hat further back on his head. "You might do that," he drawled lazily, "but it could be another day or so—if you're lucky."

"Oh, dear!"

"I suppose I could head back to the house and grab the pickup," he suggested.

It sounded like a stroke of genius to Rorie. "Would you? Listen, I'd be more than happy to pay you for your time."

He gave her an odd look. "Why would you want to do that? I'm only doing the neighborly thing."

Rorie gave him a soft smile. She'd lived in San Francisco most of her life. She loved everything about the City by the Bay, but she couldn't have named the couple in the apartment next door had her life depended on it. People in the city kept to themselves.

"By the way," he said, wiping his hands with the bright blue handkerchief, "the name's Skip. Skip Franklin."

Rorie eagerly gave him her hand, overwhelmingly grateful he'd happened along when he did. "Rorie Campbell."

"Pleased to meet you, ma'am."

"Me too, Skip."

The teenager grinned. "Now you stay right here and I'll be back before you know it." He paused, apparently considering something else. "You'll be all right here by yourself, won't you?"

"Oh, sure, don't worry about me." She braced her feet wide apart and held up her hands in the classic karate position. "I can take care of myself. I've had three self-defence lessons."

Skip chuckled, ambled toward Venture and swung up into the saddle. Within minutes he disappeared over the ridge.

Rorie watched him until he was out of sight, then she walked over to the grassy hillside and plopped herself down. The cow she'd been conversing with earlier glanced in her direction and Rorie felt obliged to explain. "He's gone for help," she called out. "Said it was the neighborly thing to do."

The heifer mooed loudly.

Rorie smiled. "I thought so, too."

An hour passed, and it seemed the longest in Rorie's life. With the sun out in full force now, she felt as if she was wilting more by the minute. Just when she began to suspect that Skip Franklin had been a figment of her overwrought imagination, she heard a loud chugging sound. She leaped to her feet and, shading her eyes with her hand, looked down the road. It was Skip, sitting atop a huge piece of farm equipment, heading in her direction.

Rorie gulped. Her gallant rescuer had come to get her on a tractor!

Skip removed his hat and waved. Even from this distance, she could see his eager grin.

Rorie feebly returned the gesture, but the smile on her lips felt brittle. Of the two modes of transportation, she would have preferred the stallion. Good grief, there was only one seat on the tractor. Where exactly did Skip plan for her to sit? On the engine?

Once the teenager reached the car, he steered the tractor in a wide circle until he faced the opposite direction from which he'd come. "Clay said we should tow the car to our place instead of leaving it on the road. You don't mind, do you?"

"Whatever he thinks is best."

"He'll be along any minute," Skip explained, jumping down from his perch. He reached for a hook and chain and began to connect the sports car to the tractor. "Clay had a couple of things he needed to do first."

Rorie nodded, grateful her options weren't so limited after all.

A couple of minutes later, the sound of another vehicle reached Rorie's ears. This time it was a late-model truck in critical need of a paint job. Rust showed through on the left front fender, which had been badly dented.

"That's Clay now," Skip announced, glancing toward the winding road.

Rorie busied herself brushing bits of grass from the skirt of her dress. When she'd finished, she looked up to see a tall muscular man sliding from the driver's side of the pickup. He was dressed in jeans and a denim shirt, and his hat was pulled low over his forehead, shading his eyes. Rorie's breath logjammed in her throat as she watched the man's grace of movement—a thoroughly masculine grace. Something about Clay Franklin grabbed hold of her imagination. He embodied everything she'd ever linked with the idea of an outdoorsman, a man's man. She could imagine him taming a wilderness or forging an empire. In his prominently defined features she sensed a strength that seemed to come from the land itself. The spellbinding quality of his steel-gray eyes drew her own and held them for a long moment. His nose was a bony protrusion with a slight curve, as though it had been broken once. He smiled, and a tingling sensation Rorie couldn't explain skittered down her spine.

His eyes still looked straight into hers and his hands rested lightly on his lean hips. "Looks like you've got yourself into something of a predicament here." His voice was low, husky—and slightly amused.

His words seemed to wrap themselves around Rorie's throat, choking off an intelligent reply. Her lips parted, but to her embarrassment no sound escaped.

Clay smiled and the fine lines that fanned out from the corners of his eyes crinkled appealingly.

"Skip thinks it might be the water pump," she said, pointing toward the MGB. The words came out weak and rusty and Rorie felt all the more foolish. She'd never had a man affect her this way. He wasn't really even handsome. Not like Dan Rogers. No, Clay wasn't the least bit like Dan, who was urbane and polished— and very proud of his neat little MGB.

"From the sounds of it, Skip's probably right." Clay walked over to the car, which his brother was connecting to the tractor. He twisted the same black hose Skip had earlier and frowned. Next he checked to see that the bumper of Dan's car was securely fastened to the chain. He nodded, lightly slapping the youths back in approval. "Nice work."

Skip beamed under his brother's praise.

"I imagine you're interested in finding a phone. There's one at the house you're welcome to use," Clay said, looking directly at Rorie.

"Thank you." Her heart pounded in her ears and her stomach felt queasy. This reaction was so unusual for her. Normally she was a calm, levelheaded twenty-four-year old, not a flighty teenager who didn't know how to act when an attractive male happened to glance in her direction.

Clay walked around to the passenger side of the pickup and held open the door. He waited for Rorie, then gave her his hand to help her climb inside. The simple action touched her heart. It had been a long time since anyone had shown her such unself-conscious courtesy.

Then Clay walked to the driver's side and hoisted himself in. He started the engine, which roared to life immediately, then shifted gears.

"I apologize for any inconvenience I've caused you," Rorie said stiffly, after several moments of silence.

"It's no problem," Clay murmured, concentrating on his driving, doing just the speed limit and not a fraction more.

They'd been driving for about ten minutes when Clay turned off the road and through a huge log archway with ELK RUN lettered across the top. Lush green pastures flanked the private road, and several horses were grazing calmly in one of them. Rorie knew next to nothing about horse breeds, but whatever type these were revealed a grace and beauty that was apparent even to her untrained eye.

The next thing Rorie noticed was the large two-story house with a wide wraparound veranda on which a white wicker swing swayed gently in the breeze. Budding rosebushes lined the meandering brick walkway.

"It's beautiful," she said softly. Rorie would have expected something like this in the bluegrass hills of Kentucky, but never on the back roads of Oregon.

Clay made no comment.

He drove past the house and around the back toward the largest stable Rorie had ever seen. The sprawling wood structure must have had room enough for thirty or more horses.

"You raise horses?" she said.

A smile moved through his eyes like a distant light. "That's one way of putting it. Elk Run is a stud farm."

"Arabians?"

"No. American Saddlebreds."

"I don't think I've ever heard of that breed before."

"Probably not," Clay said, not unkindly.

He parked the truck, helped Rorie down and then led her toward the back of the house.

"Mary," he called, holding open the screen door for Rorie to precede him into the large country kitchen. She was met with the smell of cinnamon and apples. The delectable aroma came from a freshly baked pie, cooling on the counter. A black Labrador retriever slept on a braided rug. He raised his head and thumped his tail gently when Clay stepped over to him. Absently Clay bent down to scratch the dog's ears. "This is Blue."

"Hi, Blue," Rorie said, realizing that the dog had probably been a childhood pet. He looked well advanced in years.

"Mary doesn't seem to be around."

"Mary's your wife?"

"Housekeeper," Clay informed her. "I'm not married."

That small piece of information gladdened Rorie's heart and she instantly felt foolish. Okay, so she was attracted to this man with eyes as gray as a San Francisco sky, but that didn't change anything. If her plans went according to schedule, she'd be in and out of his life within hours.

"Mary's probably upstairs," Clay explained when the housekeeper didn't immediately answer his call. "There's a phone against the wall." He pointed toward the other side of the kitchen.

While Rorie retrieved her AT&T card from her eelskin wallet, Clay crossed to the refrigerator and took out a brightly colored ceramic pitcher.

"Iced tea?" he asked.

Rorie nodded. "Please." Her throat felt parched. She had to swallow several times before she could make her call.

As she spoke on the phone, Clay took two tall glasses down from a cupboard and half-filled them with ice cubes. He poured in the tea, then added thin slices of lemon.

Rorie finished her conversation and walked over to the table. Sitting opposite Clay, she reached for the drink he'd prepared. "That was my hotel in Seattle. They won't be able to hold the room past six."

"I'm sure there'll be space in another," he said confidently.

Rorie nodded, although she thought that was unlikely. She was on her way to a writers' conference, one for which she'd paid a hefty fee, and she hated to miss one minute of it. Every hotel within a one-mile radius of the city was said to be filled.

"I'll call the garage in Nightingale for you," Clay offered.

"Is that close by?"

"About five miles down the road."

Rorie was relieved. She'd never heard of Nightingale and was grateful to hear it had a garage. After all, the place was barely large enough to rate a mention on the road map.

"Old Joe's been working on cars most of his life. He'll do a good job for you."

Once more Rorie nodded, not knowing how else to respond.

Clay quickly strode to the phone, punched out the number and talked for a few minutes. He was frowning when he replaced the receiver. Rorie wanted to question him, but before she could, he reached for an impossibly thin phone book and dialed a second number. His frown was deeper by the time he'd completed the call.

"I've got more bad news for you."

"Oh?" Rorie's heart had planted itself somewhere between her chest and her throat. She didn't like the way Clay was frowning, or the regret she heard in his voice. "What's wrong now?"

"Old Joe's gone fishing and isn't expected back this month. The mechanic in Riversdale, which is about sixty miles south of here, claims that if it is your water pump it'll take at least four days to ship a replacement."

CHAPTER TWO

"FOUR DAYS!" Rorie cried. She felt the color drain from her face. "But that's impossible! I can't possibly wait that long."

"Seems to me," Clay said in his smooth drawl, "you don't have much choice. George tells me he could have the water pump within a day if you weren't driving a foreign job."

"Surely there's someone else I could call."

Clay seemed to mull that over; then he shrugged. "Go ahead and give it a try if you like, but it isn't going to do you any good. If the shop in Riversdale can't get the part until Saturday, what makes you think someone else can do it any faster?"

Clay's calm acceptance of the situation infuriated Rorie. If she stayed four days here, in the middle of nowhere, she'd completely miss the writers' conference, which she'd been planning to attend for months. She'd scheduled her entire vacation around it. She'd made arrangements to travel to Victoria on British Columbia's Vancouver Island after the conference and on the way home take a leisurely trip down the Oregon coastline.

Clay handed her the telephone book, and feeling defeated, Rorie thumbed through the brief yellow pages until she came to the section headed Automobile

Repair. Only a handful were listed and none of them promised quick service, she noted.

"Yes, well," she muttered, expelling her breath, "there doesn't seem to be any help for it." Discouraged, she set the directory back on the counter. "You and your brother have been most helpful and I want you to know how much I appreciate everything you've done. Now if you could recommend a hotel in...what did you say was the name of the town again?"

"Nightingale."

"Right," she said, and offered him a wobbly smile, which was the best she could do at the moment. "Actually, any place that's clean will do."

Clay rubbed the side of his jaw. "I'm afraid that's going to present another problem."

"Now what? Has the manager gone fishing with Old Joe?" Rorie did her best to keep the sarcasm out of her voice, but it was difficult. Obviously the people in the community of...Nightingale, didn't take their responsibilities too seriously. If they were on the job when someone happened to need them, it was probably by pure coincidence.

"Old Joe's fishing trip isn't the problem this time," Clay explained, looking thoughtful. "Nightingale doesn't have a hotel."

"What?" Rorie exploded, slapping her hands against her legs in angry frustration. "No hotel...but there must be."

"We don't get much traffic through here. People usually stick to the freeway."

If he was implying that *she* should have done so, Rorie couldn't have agreed with him more. She might have seen some lovely scenery, but look where this little side trip had taken her! Her entire vacation was about to be ruined. Once more she slowly released her breath, trying hard to maintain her composure, which was cracking more with every passing minute.

"What about Riversdale? Surely they have a hotel?"

Clay nodded. "They do. It's a real nice one, but I suspect it's full."

"Full? I thought you just told me people don't often take this route."

"Tourists don't."

"Then how could the hotel possibly be full?"

"The Jerome family."

"I beg your pardon."

"The Jerome family is having a big reunion. People are coming from all over the country. Jed was telling me just the other day that a cousin of his is driving out from Boston. The overflow will more than likely fill up Riversdale's only hotel."

One phone call confirmed Clay's suspicion.

"Terrific," Rorie murmured, her hand still on the telephone receiver. Her tension filled the kitchen. The way things were beginning to look, she'd end up sleeping on a park bench—if Nightingale even had a park.

The back door opened and Skip wandered in, looking pleased about something. He poured himself a glass of iced tea and leaned against the counter, glancing from Rorie to Clay and then back again.

"What's happening?" he asked, when no one volunteered any information.

"Nothing much," Rorie answered. "Getting the water pump for my car is going to take four days and it seems the only hotel within a sixty-mile radius is booked full for the next two weeks and—"

"Gee, that's no problem. You can stay here," Skip inserted quickly, his blue eyes flashing with eagerness. "We'd love to have you, wouldn't we, Clay?"

Rorie spoke before the elder Franklin had an opportunity to answer. "No, really, I appreciate the offer, but I can't inconvenience you any more than I already have."

"She wouldn't be an inconvenience, would she?" Once more Skip directed his attention to his older brother. "Tell her she wouldn't be, Clay."

"It's out of the question," Rorie returned, without giving Clay the chance to echo his brother's invitation. She didn't know these people. And more important, they didn't know her and Rorie refused to impose on them further.

Clay looked into her eyes and a slow smile turned up the sensuous edges of his mouth. "It's up to you, Rorie. You're welcome on Elk Run if you want to stay."

"But you've already done so much. I really couldn't—"

"There's plenty of room," Skip announced ardently.

Those baby-blue eyes of his would melt the strongest resolve, Rorie mused.

"There's three bedrooms upstairs that are sitting empty. And you wouldn't need to worry about staying with two bachelors, because Mary's here."

It seemed inconceivable to Rorie that this family would take her in just like that. But given her options, her arguments for refusing their offer grew weaker by the minute. "You don't even know me."

"We know all we need to, don't we, Clay?" Once more Skip glanced toward his older brother, seeking his support.

"You're welcome to stay here, if you like," Clay repeated, his gaze continuing to hold Rorie's.

Again she was gripped by the compelling quality of this man. He had a jutting, stubborn jaw and she doubted there were many confrontations where he walked away a loser. She'd always prided herself on her ability to read people. And her instincts told her firmly that Clay Franklin could be trusted. She sensed he was scrupulously honest, utterly dependable—and she already knew he was generous to a fault.

"I'd be most grateful," she said, swallowing an unexpected surge of tears at the Franklins' uncomplicated kindness to a complete stranger. "But, please, let me do something to make up for all the trouble I've caused you."

"It's no trouble," Skip said, looking as though he wanted to jump up and click his heels.

Clay frowned as he watched his younger brother.

"Really," Rorie stressed. "If there's anything I can do, I'd be more than happy to lend a hand."

"I don't suppose you know anything about computers?"

"A little," she admitted hesitantly. "We've been using them at the library for several years now."

"You're a librarian?"

Rorie nodded and brushed a stray dark curl from her forehead. "I specialize in children's literature." Someday she hoped to have her own work published. That had been the reason for attending this conference in Seattle. Three of the top children's authors in the country were scheduled to speak and Rorie had so wanted to meet them. "If you have a computer system, I'd be happy to do whatever I can . . . if I can figure out how to work it."

"Clay bought one last winter," Skip informed her proudly. "He claims it's the wave of the future, the way it records horse breeding and pedigrees up to the fourth and fifth generation."

A heavyset woman Rorie assumed was the housekeeper entered the kitchen, hauling a mop and bucket. She paused to inspect Rorie with a quick measuring glance and seemed to find her lacking. She grumbled something about city girls as she sidled past Skip.

"Didn't know you'd decided to hold a convention right in the middle of my kitchen."

"Mary," Clay said, "this is Rorie Campbell, from San Francisco. Her car broke down, so she'll be staying with us for the next few days. Could you see that a bed is made up for her?"

The older woman's wide face broke into a network of frown lines.

"Oh, please, I can do that myself," Rorie said quickly. "Don't trouble yourself, Mary."

Mary nodded. "Sheets are in the closet at the top of the stairs."

"Rorie is our guest." Clay didn't raise his voice, but his displeasure was evident in every syllable.

Mary shrugged, muttering, "I got my own things to do. If the girl claims she can make a bed, then let her."

Rorie couldn't contain her smile.

"You want to invite some city slicker to stay, then fine, but I got more important matters to attend to before I make up a bed for her." With that, Mary marched out of the kitchen.

"Mary's like family," Skip explained. "It's just her nature to be sassy. She doesn't mean anything by it."

"I'm sure she doesn't," Rorie said, smiling so Clay and Skip would know she wasn't offended. She gathered that the Franklins' housekeeper didn't hold a high opinion of anyone from the city and briefly wondered why.

"I'll get your suitcase from your car," Skip offered, already heading for the door.

Clay finished off the last of his drink and set the glass on the counter. "I've got to get back to work," he said, and pausing for a moment before he added, "You won't be bored by yourself, will you?"

"Not at all. Don't worry about me."

Clay nodded. "Dinner's at six."

"I'll be ready."

Rorie picked up the empty glasses and put them by the sink. While she waited for Skip to carry in her luggage, she phoned Dan. Unfortunately he was in a meeting and couldn't be reached, so she left a message, explaining that she'd been delayed and would call again. She felt strangely reluctant to give him the Franklins' phone number, but she decided there was no reason not to do so. She also decided not to examine that feeling too closely.

Skip had returned by the time she'd hung up. "Clay says you can have Mom and Dad's old room," the teenager announced on his way through the door. He hauled her large suitcase in one hand and her flight bag was slung over his shoulder. "Their room is at the other end of the house. They were killed in an accident several years back."

"But—"

"Their room's got the best view."

"Skip, really, any bedroom will do.... I don't want your parents' room."

"But that's the one Clay wants for you." He bounded up the curving stairway with an energy reserved for the young.

Rorie followed him slowly. She slid her hand along the polished banister and glanced into the living room. A large natural-rock fireplace dominated one wall. The furniture was built of solid oak, made comfortable with thick chintz-covered cushions. Several braided rugs were strategically placed here and there on the polished wood floor. A piano with well-worn ivory keys stood to one side. The collection of family photographs displayed on top of it immediately caught her eye. She recognized a much younger Clay in what had to be his high-school graduation photo. The largest picture in an ornate brass frame was of a middle-aged couple, obviously Clay's and Skip's parents.

Skip paused at the top of the stairway and glanced over his shoulder. "My grandfather built this house over fifty years ago."

"It's magnificent."

"We think so," he admitted, eyes shining with pride.

The master bedroom, which was at the end of the hallway, opened onto a balcony that presented an unobstructed panorama of the entire valley. Rolling green pastures stretched as far as the eye could see. Rorie felt instantly drawn to this unfamiliar rural beauty. She drew a deep breath, and the thought flashed through her mind that it must be comforting to wake up to this serene landscape day after day.

"Everyone loves it here," Skip said from behind her.

"I can understand why."

"Well, I suppose I should get back to work," he said regretfully, setting her suitcases on the double bed. A colorful quilt lay folded at its foot.

Rorie slowly turned toward him, smiling. "Thank you, Skip. I hate to think what would have happened to me if you hadn't come along when you did."

He blushed and started backing out of the room, taking small steps as though he were loath to leave her. "I'll see you at dinner, okay?"

Rorie smiled again. "I'll look forward to it."

"Bye for now." He raised his right hand in a farewell gesture, then whirled around and dashed down the hallway. She could hear his feet pounding on the stairs.

It took Rorie only a few minutes to hang her things in the bare closet. When she'd finished, she went back to the kitchen where Mary was busy peeling potatoes at the stainless steel sink.

"I'd like to help, if I could."

"Fine," the housekeeper answered gruffly, as she took another potato peeler out of a nearby drawer, slapping it down on the counter. "I suppose that's your fancy sports car there in the yard."

"The water pump has to be replaced . . . I think," Rorie answered, not bothering to mention that the MGB wasn't actually hers.

"Hmph," was Mary's only response.

Rorie sighed and reached for a fat potato. "The mechanic in Riversdale said it would take until Saturday to get a replacement part."

For the second time, Mary answered her with a gruff-sounding hmph. "If then! Saturday or next Thursday or a month from now, it's all the same to George. Fact is, you could end up staying here all summer."

CHAPTER THREE

MARY'S WORDS ECHOED in Rorie's head as she joined Clay and Skip at the dinner table that evening. She stood just inside the dining room, dressed in a summer skirt and a cotton-knit cream-colored sweater, and announced, "I can't stay any longer than four days."

Clay regarded her blankly. "I have no intention of holding you prisoner, Rorie."

"I know, but Mary told me that if I'm counting on George what's-his-name to fix the MG, I could end up spending the summer here. I've got to get back to San Francisco—I have a job there." She realized how nonsensical her little speech sounded, as if that last bit about having a job explained everything.

"If you want, I'll keep after George to be sure he doesn't forget about it."

"Please." Rorie felt a little better for having spoken her mind.

"And the Greyhound bus comes through on Mondays," Skip said reassuringly. "If worse comes to worst, you could take that back to California and return later for your friend's car."

"The bus," Rorie echoed, considering the option. "I *could* take the bus." As it was, the first half of her vacation was ruined, but it'd be nice to salvage what she could of the rest.

Both men were seated, but as Rorie approached the table, Skip rose noisily to his feet, rushed around to the opposite side and pulled out a chair for her.

"Thank you," she said, smiling up at the youth. His dark hair was wet and slicked down close to his head. He'd changed out of his work clothes and into what appeared to be his Sunday best—a dress shirt, tie and pearl-gray slacks. With a good deal of ceremony, he pushed in her chair. As he leaned toward her, it was all Rorie could do to keep from grimacing at the over-powering scent of his spicy after-shave. He must have drenched himself in the stuff.

Clay's gaze tugged at hers and when Rorie glanced in his direction, she saw that he was doing his utmost to hold back a laugh. He clearly found his brother's antics amusing, though he took pains not to hurt Skip's feelings, but Rorie wasn't sure how she should react. Skip was only in his teens, and she didn't want to encourage any romantic fantasies he might have.

"I hope you're hungry," Skip said, once he'd reclaimed his chair. "Mary puts on a good feed."

"I'm starved," Rorie admitted, eyeing the numerous serving dishes spread out on the table.

Clay handed her a large platter of fried chicken. That was followed by mashed potatoes, gravy, biscuits, fresh green beans, a mixed green salad, milk and a variety of preserves. By the time they'd finished passing around the food, there wasn't any space left on Rorie's over-size plate.

"Don't forget to leave room for dessert," Clay commented, again with that slow, easy drawl of his. Here Skip was practically doing cartwheels to attract her attention and all Clay needed to do was look at her and smile and she became light-headed. Rorie couldn't understand it. From the moment Clay Franklin had stepped down from his pickup, she hadn't been the same.

"After dinner I thought I'd take you up to the stable and introduce you to King Genius," Skip said, waving a chicken leg as if conducting an orchestra.

"I'd be happy to meet him."

"Once you do, you'll feel the same way about Elk Run as you did when you stood on the balcony in the big bedroom and looked at the valley."

Obviously this King fellow wasn't a foreman, as Rorie had first assumed. More than likely, he was one of the horses she'd seen earlier grazing on the pasture in the front of the house.

"I don't think it would be a good idea to take Rorie around Hercules," Clay warned his younger brother, frowning slightly.

"Of course not." But it looked for a moment as if Skip wanted to argue.

"Who's Hercules?"

"Clay's stallion," Skip explained. "He has a tendency to act up if Clay isn't around."

Rorie could only guess what "act up" meant, but even if Skip didn't intend to heed Clay's advice, she gladly would. Other than the pony ride when she was six, Rorie hadn't been near a horse. One thing was certain, she planned to steer a wide path around the creature no matter how much Skip encouraged her. The largest pet she'd ever owned had been a guinea pig.

"When Hercules first came to Elk Run, the man who brought him claimed he was mean-spirited and untrainable. He wanted him destroyed, but Clay insisted on working with the stallion first."

"Now he's your own personal horse?" Rorie asked, directing the question to Clay.

He nodded. "We've got an understanding."

"But it's only between them," Skip added. "Hercules doesn't like anyone else getting close to him."

"He doesn't have anything to worry about as far as I'm concerned," Rorie was quick to assure both brothers. "I'll give him as much space as he needs."

Clay grinned, and once again she felt her heart turn over. This strange affinity with Clay was affirmed in the look he gave her. Unexpected thoughts of Dan Rogers sprang to mind. Dan was a divorced stockbroker she'd been seeing steadily for the past few months. Rorie enjoyed Dan's company and had recently come to believe she was falling in love with him. Now she knew differently. She couldn't be this powerfully drawn to Clay Franklin if Dan was anything more than a good friend to her. One of the reasons Rorie had decided on this vacation was to test her feelings for Dan. Two days out of San Francisco, and she had her answer.

Deliberately Rorie pulled her gaze from Clay, wanting to attribute everything she was experiencing to the clean scent of the country air.

Skip's deep blue eyes sparkled with pride as he started to tell Rorie about Elk Run's other champion horses. "But you'll love the King best. He was the five-gaited world champion four years running. Clay put him out to stud four years ago. We've been doing some crossbreeding with Arabians for the past couple of years. National Show Horses are commanding top dollar and we've produced three of the best. King's the sire, naturally."

"Do all the horses I saw in the pasture belong to you?"

"We board several," Skip answered. "Some of the others are brought here from around the country for Clay to break and train."

"You break horses?" She couldn't conceal her sudden alarm. The image of Clay sitting on a wild bronco that bucked and heaved in a furious effort to unseat him did funny things to Rorie's stomach.

"Breaking horses isn't exactly the way Hollywood pictures show it," Clay explained.

Rorie was about to ask him more when Skip planted his elbows on the table and leaned forward. Once more Rorie was assaulted by the overpowering scent of his after-shave. She did her best to smile, but if he remained in that position much longer, her eyes were sure to start watering. Already she could feel a sneeze tickling her nose.

"How old are you, Rorie?"

The question came so far out of left field that she was too surprised to answer immediately. Then she said, "Twenty-four."

Clay shot his brother a exasperated look. "Are you interviewing Rorie for the *Independent*?"

"No. I was just curious."

"She's too old for you, little brother."

"I don't know about that," Skip returned fervently. "I've always liked my women more mature. Besides, Rorie's kind of cute."

"Kind of?"

Skip shrugged. "You know what I mean. She hardly acts like a city girl."

Rorie's eyes flew from one brother to the next. They were talking as if she weren't even in the room, and that annoyed her—especially since she was the main topic of conversation.

Unaware of her reaction, Skip helped himself to another biscuit. "Actually, I thought she might be closer to twenty. With some women it's hard to tell."

"I'll take that as a compliment," Rorie muttered to no one in particular.

"I beg your pardon, Rorie," Clay said contritely. "We were being rude."

She took time buttering her biscuit. "No offense taken."

"How old do you think I am?" Skip asked her, his eyes wide and hopeful.

It was Rorie's nature to be kind, and besides, Skip had saved her from an unknown fate. "Twenty," she answered with barely a pause.

The younger Franklin straightened and sent his brother a satisfied smirk. "I was seventeen last week."

"That surprises me," Rorie continued, setting aside her butter knife and swallowing a smile. "I could have sworn you were much older."

Looking all the more pleased with himself, Skip cleared his throat. "Lots of girls think that."

"Don't I remember you saying something about helping Luke Rivers tonight?" Clay reminded his brother.

Skip's face fell. "I guess I did at that."

"If Rorie doesn't mind, I'll introduce her to King."

Clay's offer appeared to surprise Skip, and Rorie studied the boy, a little worried now about causing problems between the two brothers. Nor did she want to disappoint Skip, who had offered first.

"But I thought...." Skip began, then swallowed. "You want to take Rorie?"

Clay's eyes narrowed, and when he spoke, his voice was cool. "That's what I just said. Is there a problem with that?"

"No...of course not." Skip stuffed half a biscuit in his mouth and shook his head vigorously. After a moment of chewing, he announced, "Clay will show you around the stable." Each word was measured and even, but his gaze continued to hold his brother's.

"I heard," Rorie said gently. She could only speculate on what was going on between them, but obviously something was amiss. There had been more than a hint of surprise in Skip's eyes at Clay's offer. She noticed that the younger Franklin seemed angry. Because his vanity was bruised? Rorie supposed so. "I could wait until tomorrow if you want, Skip," she suggested.

"No, that's all right," he answered and lowered his gaze. "Clay can do it, since that's what he seems to want."

When they finished the meal, Rorie cleared the table, but Mary refused to let her help with cleaning up the kitchen.

"You'd just be in the way," she grumbled, though her eyes weren't unfriendly. "Besides, I heard something about the boys showing you the barn."

"Tomorrow night I'll do the dishes. I insist."

Mary muttered a response, then asked brusquely, "How was the apple pie?"

"Absolutely delicious."

A satisfied smile touched the edges of the housekeeper's mouth. "Good. I did things a little differently this time, and I was just wondering."

Clay led Rorie out the back door and across the yard toward the barn. The minute Rorie walked through the enormous double doors she felt she'd entered another world. The wonderful smells of leather and liniments and saddle soap mingled with the fragrance of fresh hay and the pungent odor of the horses themselves. Rorie found it surprisingly pleasant. Flashes of bright color from halters and blankets captured her attention, as did the gleam of steel bits against the far wall.

"King's over here," Clay said, guiding her with a firm hand beneath her elbow.

When Clay opened the top of the stall door, the most magnificent creature Rorie had ever seen turned to face them. He was a deep chestnut color, so sleek and powerful it took her breath away. This splendid creature seemed to know he was royalty. He regarded Rorie with a keen eye, as though he expected her to show the proper respect and curtsy. For a wild moment, Rorie was tempted to do exactly that.

"I brought a young lady for you to impress," Clay told the stallion.

King took a couple of steps back and pawed the ground.

"He really is something," Rorie whispered, once she'd found her voice. "Did you raise him from a colt?"

Clay nodded.

Rorie was about to ask him more when they heard frantic whinnying from the other side of the aisle.

Clay looked almost apologetic when he explained. "If you haven't already guessed, that's Hercules. He doesn't like being ignored." He walked to the stall opposite King's and opened the upper half of the door. Instantly the black stallion stuck his head out and complained about the lack of attention in a loud snort, which brought an involuntary smile to Rorie's mouth.

"I was bringing Rorie over to meet you, too, so don't get your neck all out of joint," Clay chastised.

"Hi," Rorie said, and raised her right hand in a stiff greeting. It amused her that Clay talked to his animals as if he honestly expected them to understand his remarks and join in the conversation. But then who was she to criticize? Only a few hours earlier, she'd been conversing with a cow.

"You don't need to be frightened of him," Clay told her when she stood, unmoving, a good distance from the stall. Taking into consideration what Skip had mentioned earlier about the moody stallion, Rorie decided to stay where she was.

Clay ran his hand down the side of Hercules's neck, a gesture that seemed to appease the stallion's obviously delicate ego.

Looking around her, Rorie was surprised by the size of the barn. "How many stalls are there all together?"

"Thirty-six regular and four foaling. But this is only a small part of Elk Run." He led her outside to a large arena and nodded at a building on the opposite side. "My office is over there, if you'd like to see it."

Rorie nodded, and they crossed to the office. Clay opened the door for her. Inside, the first thing that captured her attention was the collection of championship ribbons and photographs displayed on the walls. A large trophy case was filled with a variety of awards. When he noticed her interest in the computer, Clay explained the system he'd had installed and how it would aid him in the future.

"This is the same word-processing program we use at the library," Rorie told him.

"I've been meaning to hire a high-school kid to enter the data for me so I can get started, but I haven't got around to it yet."

Rorie sorted through the files. There were only a few hours of work and her typing skills were good. "There's no need to pay anyone. If I'm going to be imposing on your hospitality, the least I can do is type this into the system for you."

"Rorie, that isn't necessary. I don't want you to spend your time here stuck in the office doing all that tedious typing."

"It'll give me something productive to do instead of fretting over how long it's taking to get the MG repaired."

He glanced at her, his expression concerned. "All right, if you insist, but it really isn't necessary, you know."

"I do insist." Rorie clasped her hands behind her back, and decided to change the subject. "What's that?" she asked, nodding toward a large room off the office. Floor-to-ceiling windows looked out over the arena.

"The observation room."

"So you can have your own private shows?"

"In a manner of speaking. Would you like to go down there?"

"Oh, yes!"

Inside the arena, Rorie realized that it was much bigger than it had looked from above. They'd walked around for several minutes, then Clay checked his watch and frowned. "I hate to cut this short, but I've got a meeting. Normally I wouldn't leave company."

"Oh, please," she said hurriedly, "don't apologize. It's not as though I was expected or anything. I hardly consider myself company."

Still Clay looked regretful. "I'll walk you back to the house."

He left in the pickup a couple of minutes later. The house was quiet. Mary had apparently finished her duties in the kitchen and had retired to her room. Skip, who had returned from helping his friend, was busy talking on the phone. He smiled when he saw Rorie, without interrupting his conversation.

Rorie moved into the living room and idly picked up a magazine, leafing through it. Restless and bored after a few minutes, she went so far as to read a heated article on the pros and cons of a new medication used for equine worming.

When Skip was finished on the phone, he suggested they play cribbage. Not until after ten did Rorie realize she was unconsciously waiting for Clay's return. But she wasn't quite sure why.

Skip yawned rather pointedly and Rorie took the hint.

"I suppose I should think about heading up to bed," she said, putting down the deck of playing cards.

"Yeah, it seems to be that time," he answered, yawning again.

"I didn't mean to keep you up so late."

"Oh, that's no problem. It's just that we get started early around here. But you sleep in. We don't expect you to get up before the sun just because we do."

By Rorie's rough calculation, getting up before the sun meant Clay and Skip started their workday between four-thirty and five in the morning.

Skip must have read the look in her eyes, because he chuckled and said, "You get used to it."

Rorie followed him up the stairs, and they said their good-nights. But later, even after a warm bath, she couldn't sleep. Wearing her flower-sprigged cotton pajamas, she sat on the bed with the light still on and thought how everything was so different from what she'd planned. According to her schedule, she was supposed to be in Seattle now, at a cocktail party arranged for the first night of the conference; she'd hoped to talk to several of the authors there. But she'd missed that, and the likelihood of attending even one workshop was dim. Instead she'd made an unscheduled detour into a stud farm and stumbled upon a handsome rancher.

She grinned. Things could be worse. Much worse.

An hour later, Rorie heard a sound outside, behind the house. Clay must be home. She smiled, oddly pleased that he'd returned. Yawning, she reached for the lamp on the nightstand and turned it off.

The discordant noise came again.

Rorie frowned. This time, whatever was making the racket didn't sound the least bit like a pickup truck parking, or anything else she could readily identify.

Grabbing her housecoat from the foot of the bed and tucking her feet into fuzzy slippers, Rorie went downstairs to investigate.

Once she reached the kitchen she realized the clamor was coming from the barn. Trouble with the horses?

Not knowing what else to do, she raced up the stairs, taking them two at a time, and hurried from room to room until she found Skip's bedroom. She had no idea where Mary slept.

The teenager was sprawled across his bed, snoring softly.

"Skip," she cried, "something's wrong with the horses!"

He continued to snore.

"Skip," she cried, louder this time. "Wake up!"

He remained deep in sleep.

"Skip, please, oh, please, wake up!" Rorie pleaded, shaking him so hard he was sure to have bruises in the morning. "I'm from the city. Remember? I don't know what to do."

The thumps and bangs coming from the barn were growing fiercer by the minute. Perhaps there was a fire. Oh, dear Lord she prayed, not that. Rorie raced halfway down the stairs, paused, and then reversed her direction.

"Skip," she yelled. "Mary! Anyone!" Rorie heard the panic in her own voice. "Someone's got to do something!"

No one else seemed to think so.

Nearly frantic now, Rorie dashed back down the stairs and across the yard. Trembling, she entered the barn. A lone electric light shone from the ceiling, dimly illuminating the area.

Several of the Dutch stall doors were open and Rorie could sense the horses becoming increasingly restless. Walking on tiptoe, she slowly moved toward the source of the noise, somewhere in the middle of the stable. The horses were curious and their combined cries brought Rorie's heart straight to her throat.

"Nice horsey, nice horsey," she repeated soothingly over and over again until she reached the stall those unearthly sounds were coming from.

The upper half of the door was open and Rorie flattened herself against it before daring to peek inside. She saw a speckled gray mare, head thrown back and teeth bared, neighing loudly, ceaselessly. Rorie quickly jerked away and resumed her position against the outside of the door. She didn't know much about horses, but she knew this one was in dire trouble.

Racing out of the stable, Rorie picked up the hem of her housecoat and sprinted toward the house. She'd find a way to wake Skip or die trying.

She was breathless by the time she reached the yard. It was then she saw Clay's battered blue truck.

"Clay," she screamed, halting in the middle of the moonlit yard. "Oh, Clay."

He was at her side instantly, his hands roughly gripping her shoulders. "Rorie, what is it?"

She was so glad to see him, she hugged his middle and only just resisted bursting into tears. Her shoulders were heaving and her voice shook uncontrollably. "There's trouble in the barn . . . bad trouble."

CHAPTER FOUR

CLAY RACED TOWARD the barn with Rorie right behind him. He paused to flip a switch, flooding the interior with bright light.

The gray mare in the center stall continued to neigh and thrash around. Rorie found it astonishing that the walls had remained intact. The noise of the animal's pain echoed through the stable, reflected by the rising anxiety of the other horses.

Clay took one look at the mare and released a low groan, then he muttered something under his breath.

"What's wrong?" Rorie cried.

"It seems Star Bright is about to become a mother."

"But why isn't she in one of the foaling stalls?"

"Because two different vets palpated her and said she wasn't in foal."

"But . . ."

"She's already had six foals and her stomach's so stretched she looks pregnant even when she isn't." Clay opened the stall door and entered the cubicle. Rorie's hand flew to her heart. Good grief, he could get killed in there.

"What do you want me to do?" she said.

Clay shook his head. "This is no place for you. Get back to the house and stay there." His brow furrowed, every line a testament to his hard, outdoor life.

"But shouldn't I be phoning a vet or something?"

"It's too late for that."

"Boiling water—I could get that for you." She wanted to help; she just didn't know how.

"Boiling water?" he repeated. "What the hell would I need that for?"

"I don't know," she confessed lamely, "but they always seem to need it in the movies."

Clay gave an exasperated sigh. "Rorie, please, just go back to the house."

She made it all the way to the barn door, then abruptly turned back. If anyone were to ask her why she felt it so necessary to remain with Clay, she wouldn't have been able to answer. But something kept her there, something far stronger than the threat of Clay's temper.

She marched back to the center stall her head and shoulders held stiff and straight. She stood with her feet braced apart, prepared for an argument.

"Clay," she announced, "I'm not leaving."

"Listen, Rorie, you're a city girl. This isn't going to be pretty."

"I'm a woman, too. The sight of a little blood isn't enough to make me faint."

Clay was doing his best to calm the frightened mare, but without much success. The tension in the air crackled like static electricity.

"I haven't got time to argue with you," he said through clenched teeth.

"Good."

Star Bright heaved her neck backward and gave a deep groan that seemed to bounce against the sides of the stall like the boom of a cannon.

"Poor little mother," Rorie whispered in a calm soothing voice. Led by instinct, she carefully unlatched the stall door and slipped inside.

Clay sent her a look hot enough to peel paint off the wall. "Get out of here before you get hurt." His voice was low and urgent.

Star Bright reacted to his tension immediately, jerking about, her body twitching convulsively. One of her hooves caught Clay in the forearm and almost immediately, blood seeped through his sleeve. Rorie bit her lip to suppress a cry of alarm, but if Clay felt any pain, he didn't show it.

"Hold her head," Clay said sharply.

Somehow Rorie found the courage to do as he asked. Star Bright groaned once more and her pleading eyes looked directly into Rorie's, seeming to beg for help. The mare's lips pulled back from her teeth as she flailed her head to and fro, shaking Rorie in the process.

"Whoa, girl," Rorie said softly, gaining control. "It's painful, isn't it, but soon you'll have a beautiful baby to show off to the world."

"Foal," Clay corrected from behind the mare.

"A beautiful foal," Rorie repeated. She ran her hand down the sweat-dampened neck in a caressing motion, doing what she could to reassure the frightened horse.

"Keep talking," Clay whispered.

Rorie kept up a running dialogue for several tense moments, but there was only so much she could find to say on such short acquaintance. When she ran out of ideas, she started to sing in a soft, lilting voice. She began with lullabies her mother had once sung to her, then she followed those with a few childhood ditties. Her singing lasted only minutes, but Rorie's lungs felt close to collapse.

Suddenly the mare's water broke. Although Clay wasn't saying much, Rorie knew there were problems. She saw his frown, and the way he began to work furiously, though she couldn't see what he was doing. Star Bright tossed her neck in the final throes of birth and Rorie watched, fascinated, as two hooves and front legs emerged, followed by a white nose.

The mare lifted her head, eager to see. Clay tugged gently, and within seconds, the foal was free. Rorie's heart pounded like a locomotive struggling up a steep hill as Clay's strong hands completed the task.

"A filly," he announced, a smile lighting his face. He reached for a rag and wiped his hands and arms.

Star Bright turned her head to view her offspring. "See?" Rorie told the mare, her eyes moist with relief. "Didn't I tell you it would all be worth it in a little while?"

The mare nickered and her long tongue began the task of cleaning and caressing her newborn filly who was gray, like her mother, and finely marked with white streaks on her nose, mane and tail. Rorie watched, touched to her very soul by the sight. Tears blurred her vision and ran down her flushed cheeks. She wiped them aside so that Clay couldn't see them and silently chided herself for being such a sentimental fool.

It was almost another hour before they left Star Bright's stall. The mare stood guard over her long-legged baby, looking content and utterly pleased with herself. As they prepared to leave, Rorie whispered in the mare's ear.

"What was that all about?" Clay wanted to know, latching the stall door.

"I just told her she'd done a good job."

"That she did," Clay whispered. A moment later, he added, "And so did you, Rorie. I was grateful for your help."

Once more tears misted her eyes. She responded with a nod, unable to trust her voice. Her heart was racing with exhilaration. She couldn't remember a time she'd felt more excited. It was well past midnight by then, but she'd never felt less sleepy.

"Rorie?" He was watching her, his eyes bright with concern.

She owed him an explanation, although she wasn't sure she could fully explain this sudden burst of emotion. "It was so...beautiful." She brushed the dark brown hair from her face and smiled up at him, hoping he wouldn't think she was just a foolish city girl. She wasn't sure why it mattered, but she doubted that any man had seen her looking worse, although Rorie was well aware she didn't possess a classic beauty. She was usually referred to as cute, with her turned-up nose and dark brown eyes.

"I understand." He walked to the sink against the barn's opposite wall and busily washed his hands, then splashed water on his face. When he'd finished, Rorie handed him a towel hanging on a nearby hook.

"Thanks."

"I don't know how to describe it," she said, after a fruitless effort to find the words to explain all the feeling that had surged up inside her.

"It's the same for me every time I witness a birth," Clay told her. He looked at her then and gently touched her face, letting his finger glide along her jaw. All the world went still as his eyes caressed hers. There was a primitive wonder in the experience of birth, a wonder that struck deep within the soul. For the first time Rorie understood this. And sharing it with Clay seemed to intensify the attraction she already felt for him. During those few short minutes in the stall, just before Star Bright delivered her foal, Rorie felt closer to Clay than she ever had to any other man. It was as though her heart had taken flight and joined his in a moment of sheer challenge and joy. That was a silly romantic thought, she realized. But it seemed so incredible to her that she could feel anything this strong for a man she'd known for such a short time.

"I've got a name for her," Clay said, hanging up the towel. "What do you think of Nightsong?"

"Nightsong," Rorie repeated in a soft whisper. "I like it."

"In honor of the woman who sang to her mother."

Rorie nodded as emotion clogged her throat. "Does this mean I did all right for a city slicker?"

"You did more than all right."

"Thanks for not sending me away... I probably would have gone if you'd insisted."

They left the barn, and Clay draped his arm across her shoulders as though he'd been doing it for years. Rorie was grateful for his touch, because it somehow helped to ground the unfamiliar feelings and sensations.

As they strolled across the yard, she noticed that the sky was filled with a thousand glittering stars, brighter than any she could remember seeing in the city. She paused midstep to gaze up at them.

Clay's quiet voice didn't dispel the serenity. "It's a lovely night, isn't it?"

Rorie wanted to hold on to each exquisite minute and make it last a lifetime. A nod was all she could manage as she realized that this time with Clay was about to end. They would walk into the house and Clay would probably thank her for her help. Then she'd climb the stairs to her room and that would be all there was.

"How about some coffee?" he asked once they'd entered the kitchen. Blue left his rug and wandered over to Clay. "The way I feel now, it would be a waste of time to go to bed."

"For me, too." Rorie leapt at the suggestion, pleased that he wanted to delay their parting, too. And when she did return to her room, she knew the adrenaline surging through her system would make sleep impossible, anyway.

Clay was reaching up for the canister of coffee, when Rorie suddenly noticed the bloodstain on his sleeve and remembered Star Bright's kick.

"Clay, you need to take care of that cut."

From the surprised way he looked at his arm, she guessed that he, too, had forgotten about the injury. "Yes, I suppose I should." Then he calmly returned to his task.

"Let me clean it for you," Rorie offered, joining him at the kitchen counter.

"If you like." He led her into the bathroom down the hall and took a variety of medical supplies from the cabinet above the sink. "Do you want to do it here or in the kitchen?"

"Here is fine."

Clay sat on the edge of the tub and unfastened the cuff, then rolled back the sleeve.

"Oh, Clay," Rorie whispered when she saw the angry torn flesh just above his elbow. Gently her fingers tested the edges, wondering if he was going to need stitches. He winced slightly at her probing fingers.

"Sorry."

"Just put some antiseptic on it and it'll be all right."

"But this is really deep—you should probably have a doctor look at it."

"Rorie, I'm as tough as old saddle leather. This kind of thing happens all the time. I'll recover."

"I don't doubt that," she said primly.

"Then just put on a bandage and be done with it."

"But—"

"I've been injured often enough to know when a cut needs a doctor's attention."

She hesitated, then conceded that he was probably right. She filled the sink with warm tap water and took care to clean the wound thoroughly. All the while, Rorie was conscious of Clay's eyes moving over her face, solemnly perusing the chin-length, dark brown hair and the big dark eyes that still displayed a hint of vulnerability. She was tall, almost five-eight, her figure willowy. But if Clay found anything attractive about her, he didn't mention it. Her throat muscles squeezed shut, and although she was grateful for the silence between them, it confused her.

"You missed your vocation," he told her as she rinsed the bloody cloth. "You should have been a nurse."

"I toyed with the idea when I was ten, but decided I liked books better."

His shoulders were tense, Rorie noted, and she tried to be as gentle as possible. A muscle leapt in his jaw.

"I'm . . . hurting you?"

"No," he answered sharply.

After that, he was an excellent patient. He didn't complain when she dabbed on the antiseptic, although she was sure it must have stung like crazy. He cooperated when she wrapped the gauze around his arm, lifting and lowering it when she asked him to. The silence continued as she secured the bandage with adhesive tape. But Rorie had the feeling that he wanted to escape the close confines of the bathroom as quickly as possible.

"I hope that stays."

He stood up and flexed his elbow a couple of times. "It's fine. You do good work."

"I'm glad you think so."

"The coffee's probably ready by now." He spoke quickly, as if eager to be gone.

She sighed. "I could use a cup."

She put the medical supplies neatly back inside the cabinet, while Clay returned to the kitchen. Rorie could smell the freshly perked coffee even before she entered the room.

He was leaning against the counter, already sipping a cup of the fragrant coffee, waiting for her.

"It's been quite a night, hasn't it?" she murmured, adding cream and sugar to the mug he'd poured for her.

A certain tension hung in the air, and Rorie couldn't explain or understand it. Only minutes before, they'd walked across the yard, spellbound by the stars, and Clay had laid his arm across her shoulders. He'd smiled down on her so tenderly. Now he looked as if he couldn't wait to get away from her.

"Have I done something wrong?" she asked outright.

"Rorie, no." He set his mug aside and gripped her shoulders with both hands. "There's something so intimate and . . . earthy in what we shared." His eyes were tense, strangely darker. "Wanting you this way isn't right."

Rorie felt a tremor work through him as he lifted his hands to cup her face. His callused thumbs lightly caressed her cheeks.

"I feel like I've known you all my life," he whispered hoarsely, his expression uncertain.

"It's...been the same for me, from the moment you stepped out of the truck."

Clay smiled, and Rorie thought her knees would melt. She set her coffee aside and as soon as she did, Clay eased her into his arms, his hands on her shoulders and back. Her heart stopped, then jolted back to frenzied life.

"I'm going to kiss you..."

He made the statement almost a question. "I know," she whispered in return, letting him know she'd welcome his touch. Her stomach fluttered as he slowly lowered his mouth to hers.

Rorie had never wanted a man's kiss more. His moist lips glided over hers in a series of gentle explorations. He drew her closer until their bodies were pressed full length against one another.

"Oh, Rorie," he breathed, dragging his mouth from hers. "You taste like heaven...I was afraid you would." His mouth found the pulse in her throat and lingered there.

"This afternoon I wanted to cry when the car broke down and now...now I'm glad...so glad," she said.

He kissed her again, nibbling on her lower lip, gently drawing it between his teeth. Rorie could hardly breathe, her heart was pounding so hard and fast. She slumped against him, delighting in the rise and fall of his broad chest. His hands moved down her back in slow restraint, but paused when he reached the rounded curve of her hips.

He tensed. "I think we should say goodnight."

A protest sprang to her lips, but before she could voice it, Clay said. "Now."

She looked at him, dazed and uncertain. The last thing she wanted to do was leave him. "What about my coffee?"

"That was just an excuse and we both knew it."

Rorie said nothing.

The silence between them seemed to throb for endless minutes.

"Good night, Clay," she finally whispered. She broke away, but his hand caught her fingers, and with a groan he pulled her back into his arms.

"What the hell," he muttered fiercely, "sending you upstairs isn't going to help. Nothing's going to change."

His words brought confusion, but Rorie didn't question him, didn't want to. What she longed for was the warmth and security she found in his arms.

"Come on," he whispered, after his mouth had sampled hers once more. He led her through the living room and outside to the porch where the swing moved gently in the night breeze.

Rorie sat beside him and he wrapped his arm around her. She nestled her head against his shoulder, savoring these precious moments.

"I'll never forget this night."

"Neither will I," Clay promised, kissing her again.

RORIE AWOKE when the sun settled on her face and refused to leave her alone. Keeping her eyes closed, she smiled contentedly, basking in the memory of her night with Clay. They'd sat on the swing and talked for hours. Talked and kissed and laughed and touched as if they'd known each other all their lives.

Sitting up, Rorie raised her hands high above her head and stretched, arching her spine. She looked at her watch on the nightstand and was shocked to realize it was after eleven. By the time she'd climbed the stairs for bed the sky had already been dappled with faint shreds of light. She suspected Clay hadn't even bothered to sleep.

Tossing aside the blankets, Rorie slid to the floor, anxious to shower and dress. Anxious to see him again. Fifteen minutes later, she was on her way down the stairs.

Mary was dusting in the living room and glanced up when she saw Rorie. The houseckeeper grinned, then resumed her task, but not before she muttered something about how city folks were prone to sleeping their lives away.

"Good morning, Mary," Rorie greeted cheerfully.

"'Mornin'."

"Where is everyone?"

"Where they ought to be this time of the day. Working."

"Yes, I know, but where?"

"Outside."

Rorie had trouble hiding her grin.

"I heard about you helping last night," Mary added gruffly. "Seems like you did all right for a city girl."

"Thank you, Mary, you don't do half bad for a country girl, either."

The housekeeper seemed uncomfortable with the praise, despite the lightness of Rorie's tone. "I suppose you want me to cook you some fancy breakfast."

"Good heavens, no, you're busy. I'll just help myself to toast."

"That's hardly enough to fill a growing girl," Mary complained.

"It'll suit me just fine."

Once her toast was ready, Rorie carried it outside with her. If she couldn't find Clay, then she wanted to check on Nightsong.

"Rorie."

She turned to discover Skip walking toward her, in animated conversation with a blonde. His girlfriend, she guessed. He waved and Rorie returned the gesture, smiling. The sun was glorious and the day held marvelous promise.

"I didn't think you were ever going to wake up," Skip said.

"I'm sorry—I don't usually sleep this late."

"Clay told me how you helped him deliver Star Bright's filly. You could have knocked me over with a feather when I heard she was ready to foal."

Rorie nodded, her heart warming with the memory. "Well, I tried to get you up, fellow. It would have been easier to wake a dead man than to get you out of bed last night."

Skip looked slightly embarrassed. "Sorry about that, but I generally don't wake up too easily." As he spoke, he slipped his arm around the blond girl's shoulders. "Rorie, I want you to meet Kate Logan."

"Hello, Kate." Rorie held out a hand and Kate shook it politely, smiling warmly up at her.

"Hello, Rorie," she said softly. "Clay and Skip told me about your troubles. I hope everything turns out all right for you."

"I'm sure it will. Do you live around here?" Rorie already knew she was going to like her. At a closer glance, she saw that Kate was older than she'd first assumed. Maybe even close to her own age, which gave credence to Skip's comment about liking older, more mature women.

"I live pretty close," Kate explained. "The Circle L is just down the road, only a few miles from here."

"She's going to be living *with* us in the near future," Skip put in, looking fondly at Kate.

The young woman's cheeks reddened and she smiled shyly.

"Oh?" Skip couldn't possibly mean he meant to marry her, Rorie thought. Good heavens, he was still in high school.

He must have read Rorie's look, and hurried to explain. "Not me," he said with a short laugh. "Kate is Clay's fiancée."

CHAPTER FIVE

"YOU AND CLAY are engaged," Rorie murmured as shock waves coursed through her blood. They stopped with a thud at her heart and spread out in ripples of dismay. She felt as if she'd been hit by a bombshell.

Somehow Rorie managed a smile, her outward composure unbroken. She was even able to offer her congratulations. To all appearances, nothing was wrong. No one would have known that those few simple words had destroyed a night she'd planned to treasure all her life.

"I hope you and Clay will be very happy," Rorie said—and she meant it. She'd just been introduced to Kate Logan, but already Rorie knew that this sweet friendly woman was exactly the kind of wife a man like Clay would need. They were perfect for each other.

"Skip's rushing things a little," Kate pointed out, but the glint of love in her eyes contradicted her words. "Clay hasn't even given me an engagement ring yet."

"But you and Clay have been talking about getting married, haven't you?" Skip pressed. "And you're crazy about him."

Kate blushed prettily. "I've loved Clay from the time I was ten years old. I wrote his name all over my books when I was in the fifth grade. Of course, Clay wouldn't have anything to do with me, not when he was a big important high-schooler. I was just the pesky little girl next door. It took a while for him to notice me—like ten years." She gave a small laugh. "We've been dating steadily for the past two years."

"But you and Clay *are* going to get married, right?" Skip continued, clearly wanting to prove his point.

"Eventually, but we haven't set a date, although I'm sure it'll be soon," Kate answered, casting a sharp look at Rorie.

The tightness that had gripped Rorie's throat eased and she managed to keep her smile intact. It was nearly impossible not to like Kate, but that didn't lessen the ache in Rorie's heart.

"The wedding's inevitable," Skip said offhandedly, "so I wasn't exaggerating when I said you were Clay's fiancée, now was I?"

Kate smiled. "I suppose not. We love each other, and have for years. We're just waiting for the right time." Her eyes continued to hold Rorie's, assessing her, but she didn't seem worried about competition.

Rorie supposed she should be pleased about that, at least.

"I was just taking Kate over to see Nightsong," Skip explained to Rorie.

"I actually came over to Elk Run to meet you," the other woman inserted. "Clay stopped by last night and told me about your car. I felt terrible for you. Your whole vacation's been ruined. You must be awfully upset."

"Those things happen," Rorie said with a shrug. "Being upset isn't going to ship that part any faster. The only thing I can do is accept the facts."

Kate nodded, looking sympathetic. "Skip was about to show me the filly. You'll come with us, won't you?"

Rorie nodded, unable to excuse herself without sounding rude. If there'd been a way, she would have retreated, wanting only to lick her wounds in private. Instead, hoping she sounded more enthusiastic than she felt, she mumbled, "I was headed in that direction myself."

Skip led the way to the barn, which was alive with activity. Clay had explained that Elk Run employed five men full-time. Two men mucking stalls paused when Skip and the women entered the building. Skip introduced Rorie and they touched the tips of their hats in greeting.

"I just don't understand Clay," Skip said as they approached the mare's stall. "When we bought Star Bright a few years back, all Clay could do was complain about that silly name. He even toyed with the idea of getting her registration changed."

"Star Bright's a perfectly good name, I think," Kate insisted, her sunny blue eyes intent on the newborn foal.

Nightsong was standing now on knobby, skinny legs that threatened to buckle, greedily feasting from her mother.

"Oh, she really is lovely, isn't she?" Kate whispered.

Rorie hadn't been able to stop looking at the filly from the moment they'd approached the stall. Finished with her breakfast, Nightsong gazed around, fascinated by everything she surveyed. The young filly returned Rorie's look, not vacantly, but as though she recognized the woman who'd been there at her birth.

Rorie couldn't even identify all the emotions that wove their way around her heart. Some of these feelings were so new she couldn't put a name to them, but they gripped her heart and squeezed tight.

"What I can't understand," Skip muttered "is why Clay would go and name her Nightsong. It doesn't sound the least bit like anything he'd ever come up with on his own, yet he insists he did."

"I know," Kate agreed, "but I'm glad, because the name suits her." She sighed. "Clay's always been so practical when it comes to names for his horses, but Nightsong has such a sweet romantic flavor, don't you think?"

Skip chuckled. "You know what Clay thinks about romance, and that makes it all the more confusing. But Nightsong she is, and she's bound to bring us a pretty penny in a year or two. Her father was a Polish Arabian, and with Star Bright's bloodlines, Nightsong will command big bucks as a National Show Horse."

"Skip." Clay's curt voice interrupted them. He strode from the arena leading a bay mare. The horse's coat gleamed with sweat, turning its color the shade of an oak leaf in autumn. The stableman approached to take the reins. Then Clay removed his hat, wiping his brow with his forearm, and Rorie noticed the now-grimy bandage she'd applied last night. No, this morning.

She gazed hungrily at his sun-bronzed face, a face that revealed more than a hint of impatience. The carved lines around his mouth were etched deep with poorly disguised regrets. Roric recognized them, even if the others didn't.

Clay stopped short when he saw Kate, his eyes narrowing.

"Morning, Kate."

"Hello, Clay."

Then his gaze moved, slowly and reluctantly, to Rorie. The remorse she'd already sensed in him seemed to shout at her now.

"I hope you slept well," was all he said to her.

"Fine." She detected a tautness along his jaw line and decided he was probably concerned that she would do or say something to embarrass him in front of his fiancée. Rorie wouldn't, but not because she was worried about him. Her sense of fair play wouldn't allow her to hurt Kate, who so obviously adored this man.

"We're just admiring Nightsong," Kate explained, her expression tender as she gazed up at him.

"We were just talking about her, and I can't understand why you'd name her something like that," Skip said, his mouth twitching with barely suppressed laughter. "You like names like Brutus and Firepower, but Nightsong? Really, Clay, I think you may be going soft on us." Thinking himself particularly funny, Skip chuckled and added, "I suppose that's what love does to a man."

Kate's lashes brushed against the high arch of her cheek and she smiled, her pleasure so keen it was like a physical touch.

"Didn't I ask you to water the horses several hours ago?" Clay asked in a tone that could have chipped rock.

"Yes, but—"

"Then kindly see to it. The farrier will be here any minute."

The humor drained out of Skip's eyes; he was clearly upset by Clay's anger. His eyes moved from his brother to the two women and then back to Clay again. Hot color rose from his neck and invaded his face. "All right," he muttered. "Excuse me for living." Then he stormed out of the barn, slapping his hat against his thigh in an outburst of anger.

Kate waited until Skip was out of the barn. "Clay, what's wrong?"

"He should have done what I told him long before now. Those horses in the pasture are thirsty because of his incompetence."

"I'm the one you should be angry with, not Skip." Kate's voice was contrite. "I should never have stopped in this way without calling first, but I...wanted to meet Rorie."

"You've only been here a few minutes," Clay insisted, his anger in check now. "Skip had plenty of time to complete his chores before you arrived."

Rorie tossed invisible daggers at Clay. Angered at him for taking his irritation out on his younger brother. Skip had introduced her to Clay's fiancée. That was what really troubled him if he'd been willing to admit it—which he obviously wasn't.

"We came here to see Nightsong," Kate continued. "I'm glad you named her that, no matter what Skip thinks." She wrapped her arm around his waist, and rested her head against his broad chest. "He was just teasing you and you know how he loves to do that."

Clay gave her an absent smile, but his gaze settled with disturbing ease on Rorie. She met his eyes boldly, denying the emotions churning furiously in her stomach. The plea for patience and understanding he sent her was so clear, so obvious, that Rorie wondered how anyone seeing it wouldn't know what was happening.

As though she'd suddenly remembered something, Kate dropped her arm and hurriedly glanced at her watch. She hesitated and then groaned. "I promised Dad I'd meet him at lunch today. He's getting together with the other Town Council members in one of those horribly boring meetings. He needs me for an excuse to get away." She stopped abruptly, a chagrined expression on her face. "I guess that explains how informal everything is in Nightingale, doesn't it, Rorie?"

"The town seems to be doing very well." She didn't know if that was true or not, but it sounded good.

"He just hates these things, but he likes the prestige of being a Council member—something I tease him about."

"I'll walk you to your car," Clay offered.

"Oh, there's no need. You're busy. Besides I wanted to talk to Rorie and arrange to meet her tomorrow and show her around town. I certainly hope you remembered to invite her to the Grange dance tomorrow night. I'm sure Luke would be willing to escort her."

"Oh, I couldn't possibly intrude," Rorie blurted.

"Nonsense, you'd be more than welcome. And don't fret about having the right kind of clothes for a square dance, either, because I've got more outfits than I know what to do with. We're about the same size," Kate said, eyeing her. "Perhaps you're a little taller, but not so much that you couldn't wear my skirts."

Rorie smiled blandly, realizing it wouldn't do any good to decline the invitation. But good heavens, square dancing? Her?

"Knowing you and Skip," Kate chastised Clay, "poor Rorie will be stuck on Elk Run for the next four days bored out of her mind. The least I can do is see she's entertained."

"That's thoughtful of you," said Rorie, thinking that the sooner she got back on the road, the safer her heart would be, and if Kate Logan offered to help her kill time, then all the better.

"I thought I'd give you a tour of our little town in the morning," Kate went on. "It's small, but the people are friendly."

"I'd love to see Nightingale."

"Clay." The brusque voice of a farmhand interrupted them. "Could you come here a minute?"

Clay glanced at the man and nodded. "I'd better find out what Don needs," he said quietly. As he met Rorie's eyes, a speculative look flashed into his own.

She nearly flinched, wondering what emotion her face had betrayed. From the minute Clay had walked into the barn, she'd been careful to school her expression, not wanting him to read anything into her words or actions. She'd tried to look cool and unconcerned, as if the night they'd shared had never happened.

"You two will have to excuse me." Weary amusement turned up the corners of his mouth and Rorie realized he'd readily seen through her guise.

"Of course," Kate said. "I'll see you later, sweetheart."

Clay nodded abruptly and departed with firm purposeful strides.

Kate started walking toward the yard. Rorie followed, eager to escape the barn and all the memories associated with it.

"Clay told us you're a librarian," Kate said when she reached the Ford parked in the curving driveway. "If you want, I can take you to our library. We built a new one last year and we're rather proud of it. I know it's small compared to where you probably work, but I think you'll like what we've done."

"I'd love to see it." Libraries were often the heart of a community, and if the good citizens of Nightingale had seen fit to pay tax dollars to upgrade theirs, then it was apparent they shared Rorie's love of literature.

"I'll pick you up around ten tomorrow, if that's convenient?"

"That'd be fine."

"Plan on spending the afternoon with me and we'll meet Clay and Skip at the dance later."

Rorie agreed, although her enthusiasm was decidedly low. How Dan would tease her if he ever discovered she'd spent part of her vacation square dancing with the folks at the Grange.

"'Bye for now," Kate said.

"'Bye," Rorie murmured waving. She stood in the yard until Kate's car was out of sight. Not knowing what else to do, she wandered back into the house, where Mary was busy with preparations for lunch.

"Can I help?" she asked.

In response, Mary scurried to a drawer and once again handed her a peeler. Rorie started carefully whittling away at a firm red apple she'd scooped from a large bowlful of them.

"I don't suppose you know anything about cooking?" Mary demanded, pointing her own peeler at Rorie.

"I've managed to keep from starving the last several years," she retorted idly.

The merest hint of amusement flashed into the older woman's weathered face. "If I was judging your talents in the kitchen on looks alone, I think you'd starve a man to death within a week."

Despite her glum spirits, Rorie laughed. "If you're telling me you think I'm thin, watch out, Mary, because I'm likely to throw my arms around your neck and kiss you."

The other woman chanced a grin at that. A few peaceful minutes passed while they pared apple after apple.

"I got a call from my sister," Mary said hesitantly, her eyes darting to Rorie, then back to her task. "She's coming as far as Riversdale and wants to know if I can drive over and see her. She's only going to be in Oregon one day."

This was the most Mary had said to Rorie since her arrival. The realization pleased her. The older woman was lowering her guard and extending a friendly hand.

"I'd like to visit with my sister."

"I certainly think you should." It took Rorie another minute to figure out where Mary was directing this meandering conversation. Then suddenly she understood. "Oh, you're looking for someone to do the cooking while you're away."

Mary shrugged as if it didn't concern her one way or the other. "Just for one meal, two nights from now. I could manage lunch for the hands before I leave. It's the evening meal I'm worried about. There's only Clay and Skip who need to be fed—the other men go home in the evenings."

"Well, relax, because I'm sure I can manage one dinner without killing off the menfolk."

"You're sure?"

Mary was so completely serious that Rorie laughed outright. "Since my abilities do seem to worry you, how would you feel if I invited Kate Logan over to help?"

Mary nodded and sighed. "I'd rest easier."

RORIE STAYED in the kitchen until the lunch dishes had been washed and put away. Mary thanked her for the help, then went into her bedroom to watch her daily soap operas.

Feeling a little lost, Rorie wandered outside and into the stable. Since Clay had already shown her the computer, she decided to spend the afternoon working in his office.

The area was deserted, which went some distance toward reassuring her—but then, she'd assumed it would be. From what she'd observed, a stud farm was a busy place and Clay was bound to be occupied elsewhere. That suited Rorie just fine. She hoped to avoid him as much as possible. In three days she'd be out of his life, leaving hardly a trace, and that was the way she wanted it.

Rorie sat typing in data for about an hour before her neck and shoulders began to develop a cramp. She paused, flexing her muscles, then rotated her head to relieve the building tightness.

"How long have you been in here?"

The rough male voice behind her startled Rorie. Her hand flew to her heart and she expelled a shaky breath. "Clay! Good heavens, you frightened me."

"How long?" he repeated.

"An hour or so." She glanced at her watch and nodded.

Clay advanced a step toward her, his mouth a thin line of impatience. "I suppose you're looking for an apology."

Rorie didn't answer. She'd learned not to expect anything from him.

"I'm here to tell you right now that you're not going to get one," he finished gruffly.

CHAPTER SIX

"You don't owe me anything, Clay," Rorie said, struggling to make her voice light. Clay looked driven to the limits of exhaustion. Dark shadows had formed beneath his eyes and fatigue lines fanned out from their corners. His shoulders sagged slightly, as if the weight he carried was more than he could bear. He studied her wearily, then turned away from her, stalking to the other side of the office. His shoulders heaved as he drew in a shuddering breath.

"I know I should feel some regrets, but God help me, Rorie I don't."

"Clay, listen..."

He turned to face her then, and drove his fingers into his hair with such force Rorie winced. "I'd like to explain about Kate and me."

"No." The last thing Rorie wanted was to be forced to listen to his explanations or excuses. She didn't have a lot of room to be judgmental. She herself had, after all, been dating a man steadily for the past few months. "Don't. Please don't say anything. It isn't necessary."

He ignored her request. "Kate and I have known each other all our lives."

"Clay, stop." She pushed out the chair and stood up, wanting only to escape, and knowing she couldn't.

"For the last two years, it's been understood by everyone around us that Kate and I would eventually get married. I didn't even question the right or wrong of it, just calmly accepted the fact. A man needs someone to share his life.''

"Kate will make you a wonderful wife," she said forcefully, feeling both disillusioned and indignant, but she refused to let him know how much his small indiscretion had hurt her. "If you owe anyone an apology, it's Kate, not me."

His responding frown was brooding and dark. "I know." He drew his fingers across his eyes, and she could feel his exhaustion from the other side of the room. "The last thing in the world I want is to hurt Kate."

"Then don't."

He stared at her, and Rorie forced herself to send him a smile, although she feared it was more flippant than reassuring. "There's no reason for Kate to know. What good would it do? She'd only end up feeling betrayed. Last night was a tiny impropriety and best forgotten, don't you agree?" Walking seemed to help, and Rorie paced the office, her fingers brushing the stack of books and papers on his cluttered desk.

"I don't know what's best anymore," Clay admitted quietly.

"I do," Rorie said with unwavering confidence, still struggling to make light of the incident. "Think about it, Clay. We were alone together for hours—we shared something beautiful with Star Bright and . . . her foal. And we shared a few stolen kisses under the stars. If anything's to blame, I think it should be the moonlight. We're strangers, Clay. You don't know me and I don't know you." Afraid to look him directly in the eye, Rorie lowered her gaze and waited, breathless, for his next words.

"So it was the moonlight?" His voice was hoarse and painfully raw.

"Of course," she lied. "What else could it have been?"

"Yes, what else could it have been?" he echoed, then turned and walked out of the office.

It suddenly seemed as though the room's light had dimmed. Rorie felt so weak, she sank into the chair, shocked by how deeply the encounter had disturbed her.

Typing proved to be a distraction and Rorie left the office a couple of hours later with a feeling of accomplishment. She'd been able to enter several time-consuming pages of data into the computer system. The routine mechanical work was a relief because it didn't give her time to think. Sorting through her thoughts could be dangerous.

The kitchen smelled of roasting beef and simmering apple crisp when Rorie let herself in the back door. It was an oddly pleasant combination of scents. Mary was nowhere to be seen.

While she remembered, Rorie reached for the telephone book and dialed the number listed for the garage in Riversdale.

"Hello," she said abruptly when a gruff male voice answered. "This is Rorie Campbell...the woman with the broken water pump. The one in Nightingale."

"Yeah, Miss Campbell, what can I do for you?"

"I just wanted to be sure there wasn't any problem in ordering the part. I don't know if Clay...Mr. Franklin told you, but I'm more or less stuck here until the car's repaired. I'd like to get back on the road as soon as possible—I'm sure you understand."

"Lady, I can't make that water pump come any faster than what it already is."

"I know, but I just wanted to check and be sure you'd been able to order one."

"It's on its way, at least that's what the guy in Los Angeles told me. They're shipping it by overnight freight to Portland. I've arranged for a man to pick it up the following day, but it's going to take him some time to get it to me."

"But that's only three days."

"You called too late yesterday for me to phone the order in. Lady, there's only so much I can do."

"I know, I'm sorry if I sound impatient."

"The whole world's impatient. Listen, I'll let you know the minute it arrives."

She sighed. "Thanks, I'd appreciate it."

"Clay got your car here without a hitch, so you don't need to worry about that—he saved you a bundle on towing charges. Shipping costs and long-distance phone bills are going to be plenty high, though."

Rorie hadn't even noticed that Dan's shiny sports car wasn't in the yard where Skip had originally left it. "So you'll be calling me within the next day or two?" she asked, trying to hide the anxiety in her voice. And trying not to think about the state of her finances, already depleted by this disastrous vacation.

"Right. I'll call as soon as it comes in."

"Thank you. I appreciate it more than I can say."

"No problem," the mechanic muttered, obviously eager to end their conversation.

When the call was finished, Rorie toyed with the idea of phoning Dan next. She'd been half expecting to hear from him, since she'd left the Franklins' number with his secretary the day before. He hadn't phoned her back. But there wasn't anything new to tell him, so she decided not to call a second time.

Hesitantly Rorie replaced the telephone receiver, pleased that everything was under control—everything except her heart.

DINNER THAT EVENING was a strained affair. If it hadn't been for Skip, who seemed oblivious to the tension between her and Clay, Rorie didn't think she could have endured it. Clay hardly said a word throughout the meal. But Skip seemed more than eager to carry the conversation and Rorie did her best to lighten the mood, wondering all the time whether Clay saw through her facade.

"While you're here, Rorie," Skip said with a sudden burst of enthusiasm, "you should think about learning to ride."

"No, thank you," she said pointedly, holding up her hand, as though fending off the suggestion. A mere introduction to King and Hercules was as far as she was willing to go.

"Rain Magic would suit you nicely."

"Rain Magic?"

"That's a silly name Kate thought up, and Clay went along with it," Skip explained. "He's gentle, but smart—the gelding I mean, not Clay." The younger Franklin needled his older brother, then laughed heartily at his own attempt at humor.

Clay smiled, but Rorie wasn't fooled; he hadn't been amused by the joke, nor, she suspected, was he pleased by the reference to Kate.

"No thanks, Skip," she said, before the subject could get out of control. "I'm really not interested." There, that said it plain enough.

"Are you afraid?"

"A little," she admitted truthfully. "I prefer all my horses on a merry-go-around, thank you. I'm a city girl, remember?"

"But even girls from San Francisco have been known to climb on the back of a horse. It'll be good for you, Rorie. Trust me—it's time to broaden your horizons."

"Thanks, but no thanks," she told him, emphasizing her point by biting down on a crisp carrot stick. The loud crunch added an exclamation point to her words.

"Rorie, I insist. You aren't going to get hurt—I wouldn't let that happen, and Rain Magic is as gentle as they come. In fact—" he wiggled his eyebrows up and down several times "—if you want, we can ride double until you feel more secure."

Rorie laughed. "Skip, honestly."

"All right, you can ride alone, and I'll lead you around in a circle. For as long as you want."

Rorie shook her head and, amused at the mental picture that scenario presented, laughed again.

"Leave it," Clay said with sudden sharpness. "If Rorie doesn't want to ride, that should be the end of it."

Skip's shocked gaze flew from Rorie to his brother. "I was just having a little fun, Clay."

His older brother gripped his water goblet so hard that Rorie feared the glass would shatter. "Enough is enough. She said she wasn't interested in learning to ride and that should be the end of it."

The astounded look left Skip's features, but his eyes narrowed and he stiffened his shoulders in a display of righteous indignation. "What's with you, Clay?" he shouted. "You've been acting like a wounded bear all day, barking and biting at everyone. Who declared you king of the universe all of a sudden?"

"If you'll excuse me, I'll bring in the apple crisp," Rorie said, and hurriedly rose to her feet, not wanting to be caught in the crossfire between the two brothers. Whatever they had to say wasn't meant for her ears.

The exchange that followed ended quickly, Rorie noted gratefully from inside the kitchen. Their voices were raised and then there was a sudden hush followed by laughter. Rorie relaxed and picked up the dessert, carrying it into the dining room along with a carton of vanilla ice cream.

"I apologize, Rorie," Clay said soberly when she reentered the room. "Skip's right, I've been cross and unreasonable all day. I hope my sour mood hasn't ruined your dinner."

"Of course not," she murmured, offering him a smile.

Clay stood up to serve the dessert dishes, spooning generous helpings of apple crisp and ice cream in each bowl.

Skip chattered aimlessly, commenting on one subject and then bouncing to another without any logical connection, his thoughts darting this way and that.

"What time are you going over to Kate's tonight?" he asked Clay casually.

"I won't be. She's got some meeting with the women's group from the Grange. They're doing decorations for the dance tomorrow night."

"Now that you mention it, I seem to remember Kate saying something about being busy tonight, too." Without any pause he turned to Rorie. "You'll be coming, I hope. The Grange is putting on a square dance—the biggest one of the year and they usually do it up good."

"Kate already invited me. I'll be going with her," Rorie explained, although she hadn't the slightest idea how to square dance. Generally she enjoyed dancing although she hadn't done any for several months because Dan wasn't keen on it.

"You could drive there with us if you wanted," Skip offered. "I'd kinda like to walk in there with you on my arm. I know you'd cause quite a stir with the men, especially with Luke Rivers—he's the foreman at the Logan place. Most girls go all goo-goo-eyed over him."

Clay's spoon clanged loudly against the side of his glass dish and he murmured an apology.

"I'm sorry, Skip," Rorie said gently, "I already told Kate I'd drive over with her."

"Darn," Skip muttered.

The rest of the meal was completed in silence. Once, when Rorie happened to glance up, her gaze collided with Clay's. Her heart felt as though it might hammer its way out of her chest. She was oppressively aware of the chemistry between them. It simmered in Rorie's veins and she could tell that Clay felt everything she did. Throughout dinner, she'd been all too conscious of the swift stolen glances Clay had sent in her direction. She sent a few of her own, though she'd tried hard not to. But it was impossible to be in the same room with this man and not react to him.

A thousand times in the next couple of hours, Rorie told herself everything would be fine as soon as she could leave. Life would return to normal then.

After the dishes were finished, Skip challenged her to a game of cribbage, and grateful for the escape, Rorie accepted. Skip sat with his back to his brother, and every time Rorie played her hand, she found her gaze wandering across the room to where Clay sat reading.

To all outward appearances, he was relaxed and comfortable, but she knew he felt as tense as she did. She knew he was equally aware of the electricity that sparked between them.

Rorie's fingers shook as she counted out her cards.

"Fifteen eight," Skip corrected. "You forgot two points."

Her eyes fell to the extra ten, and she blinked. "I guess I did."

Skip heaved a sigh. "I don't think your mind's on the game tonight."

"I guess not," she admitted wryly. "If you don't mind, I think I'll head up to bed." She offered him an apologetic smile and reached for her coffee cup. Skip was right. Her mind hadn't been on the game at all. Her thoughts had been centered on a man who owed his loyalties to another woman—a woman whose roots were intricately bound with his. A woman Rorie had liked and respected from the moment they met.

Feeling depressed, she bade the two men good night and carried her cup into the kitchen. Dutifully, she rinsed it out and set it beside the sink, but when she turned around Clay was standing in the doorway, blocking her exit.

"Where's Skip?" she asked a little breathlessly. Heat seemed to throb between them and she retreated a step in a futile effort to escape.

"He went upstairs."

She blinked and faked a yawn. "I was headed in that direction myself."

Clay buried one hand in his jeans pocket. "Do you know what happened tonight at dinner?"

Not finding her voice, Rorie shook her head.

"I was jealous," he said between clenched teeth. "You were laughing and joking with Skip and I wanted it to be me your eyes were shining for. Me. No one else." He stopped abruptly and shook his head. "Jealous of a seventeen-year-old boy...I can't believe it myself."

CHAPTER SEVEN

NOT KNOWING what to expect, Rorie decided to wear a dress for her outing with Kate Logan. Although she rose early, both Skip and Clay had eaten breakfast and left the house by the time she came downstairs. Which was just as well, Rorie thought.

Mary stood at the stove, frying chunks of beef for a luncheon stew. "I spoke to Clay about you cooking dinner later this week. He says that'll be fine if you're still around, but the way he sees it, you'll be headed north within a day or two."

Rorie poured herself a cup of coffee. "I'll be happy to do it if I'm here. Otherwise, I'm sure Kate Logan would be more than pleased."

Mary turned to face her, mouth open as if to comment. Instead her eyes widened in appreciation. "My, my, you look pretty enough to hog-tie a man's heart."

"Thank you, Mary," Rorie answered, grinning.

"I suppose you got yourself a sweetheart back there in San Francisco?" she asked, watching her closely. "A pretty girl like you is bound to attract plenty of men."

Rorie paused to consider her answer. She thought briefly about mentioning Dan, but quickly decided against it. She'd planned this separation to gain a perspective on their relationship. And within hours of arriving at Elk Run, Rorie had found her answer. Dan would always be a special friend—but nothing more.

"The question shouldn't require a week's thought," Mary grumbled, stirring the large pot of simmering beef.

"Sorry... I was just mulling something over."

"Then there is someone special?"

She shook her head lightly. "No."

The answer didn't seem to please Mary, because she frowned. "When did you say that fancy car of yours was going to be fixed?"

The abrupt question caught Rorie by surprise. Mary was openly concerned about the attraction between her and Clay. The housekeeper, who probably knew Clay better than anyone, clearly wasn't blind to what had been happening—and just as clearly, didn't like it.

"The mechanic in Riversdale said it should be finished the day after tomorrow if all goes well."

"Good!" Mary proclaimed with a fierce nod, then turned back to her stew.

Rorie couldn't help grinning at the older woman's astuteness. Mary was telling her that the sooner she was off Elk Run the better for everyone concerned. In truth, Rorie couldn't agree with her more.

Kate Logan arrived promptly at ten. She wore tight-fitting jeans, red checkered western shirt and a white silk scarf knotted at her throat. Her long honey-colored hair was woven into thick braids that fell over her shoulders. At first glance, Kate looked closer to sixteen than the twenty-four Rorie knew her to be.

Kate greeted her with a warm smile. "Rorie, there wasn't any need to wear something so nice. I should have told you to dress casually."

Rorie's shoulders slumped. "I brought along more dresses than jeans. Am I really overdressed? I could change," she said hesitantly.

"Oh, no, you look fine...more than fine." But for the first time, Kate sounded worried. The doubt that played across her features would have been amusing if Rorie hadn't already been suffering from such a potent bout of guilt. It was all too clear that Kate viewed Rorie as a threat.

If Clay Franklin had chosen that moment to walk into the kitchen, Rorie would have turned on him, calling him every foul name she could think of. She was furious with him for doing this to her—and to Kate.

"I wear a lot of dresses because of my job at the library." Rorie rushed to explain. "I also date quite a bit. I've been seeing someone—Dan Rogers—for months now. In fact, it's his car I was driving."

"You're dating someone special?" Kate asked, looking relieved.

"Yes, Dan and I've been going together for several months."

Mary coughed noisily and threw Rorie an accusing glare; Rorie ignored her. "Shouldn't we be leaving?"

"Oh sure, any time you're ready." When they were outside, Kate turned to face Rorie. Looking uncomfortable, she slipped her hands into the back pockets of her jeans. "I've embarrassed you and I apologize. I didn't mean to imply that I didn't trust you and Clay."

"There's no need for an apology, really. I'm sure I wouldn't feel any differently if Clay were my fiancé."

Kate shook her head. "But I feel like I *should* apologize. I'm not going to be the kind of wife Clay wants if I can't trust him around a pretty girl once in a while."

Had the earth cracked open just then, Rorie would gladly have fallen in. That had to be better than looking at Kate and feeling the things she did about Clay Franklin.

"Don't have any worries about me," she said lightly, dismissing the issue as nonchalantly as she could. "I'll be out of everyone's hair in a day or two."

"Oh, Rorie, please, I don't mean for you to rush off because I had a silly attack of jealousy. Now I feel terrible."

"Don't please. I have to leave . . . I want to leave. My vacation's on hold until I can get my car repaired and there's so much I'd planned to see and do." She dug in her purse for a brochure she'd been carrying with her. "Have you ever been up to Victoria on Vancouver Island?"

"Once, but I was only five, much too young to remember much of anything," Kate told her, scanning the pamphlet. "This does sound like a fun trip. It sounds like just the place Clay and I should honeymoon."

"It'd be perfect for that," Rorie murmured. Her heart constricted on a sudden flash of pain, but she ruthlessly forced down her emotions, praying Kate hadn't noticed. "I'm looking forward to visiting Canada. By the way, Mary's driving to Riversdale to visit her sister later in the week. She's asked me to take charge of cooking dinner if I'm still here. Would you like to help? We could have a good time and get to know each other better."

"Oh, that sounds great." Kate slipped her arm around Rorie's trim waist and gave her an enthusiastic squeeze. "Thank you, Rorie. I know you're trying to reassure me, and I appreciate it."

That had been exactly Rorie's intent.

"It probably sounds selfish," Kate continued, "but I'm glad your car broke down when it did. Without any difficulty at all, I can see us becoming the best of friends."

Rorie could, too, but it only added to her growing sense of uneasiness.

NIGHTINGALE WAS a sleepy kind of town. Businesses lined both sides of Main Street, with a beauty shop, an insurance agency, Nellie's Café and a service station on one side, a grocery store, pharmacy and five-and-dime on the other. Rorie had the impression that things happened in their own good time in Nightingale. Few places could have been more unlike San Francisco, where people always seemed to be rushing, always scurrying from one spot to another. Here, no one seemed to feel any need to bustle. It was as though this town, with its population of fifteen hundred, existed in a time warp. Rorie found the relaxed pace unexpectedly pleasant.

"The library is across from the high school on Maple Street," Kate explained as she parked her Ford on Main. "That way, students have easy access to the building."

Rorie climbed out of the car, automatically pressing down the door lock.

"You don't need to do that here. There hasn't been a vehicle stolen in . . . oh, at least twenty years."

Rorie's eyes must have revealed her surprise, because Kate added, "Actually, we had trouble passing our last bond issue for a new patrol car. People couldn't see the need since there hasn't been a felony committed here in over two years. About the worst thing that goes on is when Harry Ackerman gets drunk. That happens once or twice a year and he's arrested for disturbing the peace." She paused and grinned sheepishly. "He sings old love songs to Nellie at the top of his lungs in front of the café. They were apparently sweet on each other a long time back. Nellie married someone else and Harry never got over the loss of his one true love.''

Looping the strap of her purse over her shoulder, Rorie looked around the quiet streets.

"The fire and police station are in the same building," Kate pointed out next. "And the one really nice restaurant is on Oak. If you want, we could have lunch there."

"Only if you let me treat."

"I wouldn't hear of it," Kate insisted with a shake of her head that sent her braids flying. "You're my guest."

Rorie decided not to argue, asking another question instead. "Where do the ranchers get their supplies?" It seemed to her that type of store would do a thriving business, yet she hadn't seen one.

"At Garner's Feed and Supply. It's on the outskirts of town—I'll take you past on the way out. In fact, we should take a driving tour so you can see a little more of the town. Main Street is only a small part of Nightingale."

By the time Kate and Rorie walked over to Maple and the library, Rorie's head was swimming with the names of all the people Kate had insisted on introducing. It seemed that everyone had heard about her car problems and was eager to talk to her. Several mentioned the Grange dance that night and said they'd be looking for her there.

"You're really going to be impressed with the library," Kate promised as they walked the two streets over to Maple. "Dad and the others worked hard to get the levy passed so we could build it. People here tend to be tightfisted. Dad says they squeeze a nickel so hard, the buffalo belches."

Rorie laughed outright at that.

The library was the largest building in town, a sprawling one-story structure with lots of windows. The hours were posted on the double glass doors, and Rorie noted that the library wouldn't open until the middle of the afternoon, still several hours away.

"It doesn't look open," she said disappointed.

"Oh, don't worry, I've got a key. All the volunteers do." Kate rummaged in her bag and took out a large key ring. She opened the door, pushing it wide for Rorie to enter first.

"Mrs. Halldorfson retired last year, a month after the building was finished," Kate told her, flipping on the lights, "and the town's budget wouldn't stretch to hire a new full-time librarian. So several parents and teachers are taking turns volunteering. We've got a workable schedule, unless someone goes on vacation, which, I hate to admit, has been happening all summer."

"You don't have a full-time librarian?" Rorie couldn't disguise her astonishment. "Why go to all the trouble and expense of building a modern facility if you can't afford a librarian?"

"You'll have to ask Town Council that," Kate returned, shrugging. "It doesn't make much sense, does it? But you see, Mrs. Halldorfson was only part-time and the Council seems to think that's what her replacement should be."

"That doesn't make sense, either."

"Especially when you consider that the new library is twice the size of the old one."

Rorie had to bite her tongue to keep from saying more. But she was appalled at the waste, the missed opportunities.

"We've been advertising for months for a part-time librarian, but so far we haven't found anyone interested. Not that I blame them—one look at the size of the job and no one wants to tackle it alone.''

"A library is more than a place to check books in and out," Rorie insisted, gesturing dramatically. Her voice rose despite herself. This was an issue close to her heart, and polite silence was practically impossible. "A library can be the heart of a community. It can be a place for classes, community services, all kinds of things. Don't non-profit organizations use it for meetings?''

"I'm afraid not," Kate answered. "Everyone gets together at Nellie's when there's any kind of meeting. Nellie serves great pies," she added, as though that explained everything.

Realizing that she'd climbed to her soapbox, Rorie dropped her hands an shrugged. "It's a very nice building, Kate, and you have every reason to be proud. I didn't mean to sound so righteous.''

"But you're absolutely correct," Kate said thoughtfully "We're not using the library to it's full potential, are we? Volunteers can only do so much. As it is, the library's only open three afternoons a week." She sighed expressively. "To be honest, I think Dad and the other members of the Town Council are expecting Mrs. Halldorfson to come back in the fall, but that's unfair to her. She's served the community for over twenty years. She deserves to retire in peace without being blackmailed into coming back because we can't find a replacement.''

"Well I hope you find someone soon."

"I hope so, too," Kate murmured.

They ate a leisurely lunch, and as she'd promised, Kate gave Rorie a brief tour of the town. After pointing out several churches, the elementary school where she taught second grade and some of the nicer homes on the hill, Kate ended the tour on the outskirts of town near Garner's Feed and Supply.

"Luke's here," Kate explained, easing into the parking place next to a dusty pickup truck.

"Luke?"

"Our foreman. I don't know what Dad would do without him. He runs the ranch and has for years—ever since I was in high school. Dad's retirement age now, and he's more than willing to let Luke take charge of things."

Kate got out of the car and leaned against the front fender, crossing her arms over her chest. Not knowing what else to do, Rorie joined her there.

"He'll be out in a minute," Kate explained.

True to her word a tall, deeply tanned man appeared with a sack of grain slung over his shoulder. His eyes were so dark they gleamed like onyx, taking in everything around him, but revealing little of his own thoughts. His strong square chin was balanced by a high intelligent brow. He was lean and muscular and strikingly handsome.

"Need any help, stranger?" Kate asked with a light laugh.

"You offering?"

"Nope."

Luke chuckled. "I thought not. You wouldn't want to ruin those pretty nails of yours now, would you?"

"I didn't stop by to be insulted by you," Kate chastised, clearly enjoying the exchange. "I wanted you to meet Rorie Campbell—she's the one Clay was telling us about the other night, whose car broke down."

"I remember." For the first time the foreman's gaze drifted from Kate. He tossed the sack of grain into the back of the truck and used his teeth to tug his glove free from his right hand. Then he presented his long callused fingers to Rorie. "Pleased to meet you, ma'am."

"The pleasure's mine." Rorie remembered where she'd heard the name. Skip had mentioned Luke Rivers when he'd told her about the Grange square dance. He'd said something about all the girls being attracted to the Logan foreman. Rorie could understand why.

They exchanged a brief handshake before Luke's attention slid back to Kate. His eyes softened perceptibly.

"Luke's like a brother to me," Kate said fondly.

He frowned at that, but didn't comment.

"We're going to let you escort us to the dance tonight," she informed him.

"What about Clay?"

"Oh, he'll be by. I thought the four of us could go over together."

Rorie wasn't fooled. Kate was setting her up with Luke, who didn't look any too pleased at having his evening arranged for him.

"Kate, listen," she began, "I'd really rather skip the dance tonight. I've never done square dancing in my life—"

"That doesn't matter," Kate interrupted. "Luke will be glad to show you. Won't you Luke?"

"Sure," he mumbled, with the enthusiasm of a man offered the choice between hanging and a firing squad.

"Honestly, Luke!" Kate gave an embarrassed laugh.

"Listen," Rorie said quickly. "It's obvious Luke has his own plans for tonight. I don't want to intrude—"

He surprised her by turning toward her, his eyes searching hers. "I'd be happy to escort you, Rorie."

"I'm likely to step all over your toes . . . I really think I'd do best to sit the whole thing out."

"Nonsense," Kate cried. "Luke won't let you do that and neither will I!"

"We'll have a good time," the foreman insisted. "Leave everything to me."

Rorie nodded, although she felt little enthusiasm.

A moment of awkward silence fell over the trio. "Well, I suppose I should get Rorie back to Circle L and see about finding her a dress," Kate said, smiling. She playfully tossed her car keys into the air and caught them deftly.

Luke tipped his hat when they both returned to the car. Rorie didn't mention his name until they were back on the road.

"He really is attractive, isn't he?" she asked, closely watching Kate.

The other woman nodded eagerly. "It surprises me that he hasn't married. There are plenty of girls around Nightingale who would be more than willing, believe me. At every Grange dance, the ladies flirt with him like crazy. I love to tease him about it—he really hates that. But I wish Luke *would* get married—I don't like the idea of him living his life alone. It's time he thought about settling down and starting a family. He was thirty last month, but the last time I mentioned it to him, he nearly bit my head off."

Rorie nibbled on her lower lip. She inhaled a deep breath and released it slowly. Her guess was that Luke had his heart set on someone special, and that someone was engaged to another man. God help him, Rorie thought. She knew exactly how he felt.

THE MUSIC WAS ALREADY playing by the time Luke, Kate and Rorie arrived a the Grange Hall in Luke's ten-year-old four-door sedan. Rorie tried to force some enthusiasm for this outing, but had little success. She hadn't exchanged more than a few words with the Logan foreman during the entire drive. He, apparently, didn't like this arranged-date business any better than she did. But they were stuck with each other, and Rorie at least was determined to make the best of it.

They entered the hall and were greeted with the cheery sounds of the male caller:

Rope the cow, brand the calf
Swing your sweetheart, once and a half...

Rorie hadn't known what to expect, but she was surprised by the smooth-stepping, smartly dressed dancers who twirled around the floor following the caller's directions. She felt more daunted than ever by the evening ahead of her. And to worsen matters, Kate had insisted Rorie borrow one of her outfits. Although Rorie liked the bright blue colors of the western skirt and matching blouse, she felt awkward and self-conscious in the billowing skirts.

The Grange itself was bigger than Rorie had anticipated. On the stage stood the caller and several fiddlers. Refreshment tables lined one wall and the polished dance floor was so crowded Rorie found it a wonder that anyone could move without bumping into others. The entire meeting hall was alive with energy and music, and despite herself, she felt her mood lift. Her toes started tapping out rhythms almost of their own accord. Given time, she knew she'd be out there, too, joining the vibrant, laughing dancers. It was unavoidable, anyway. She knew Kate, Clay and Skip weren't going to allow her to sit sedately in the background and watch.

"Oh, my feet are moving already," Kate cried, squirming with eagerness. Clay smiled indulgently, tucked his arm around her waist and the two of them stepped onto the dance floor. He glanced back once at Rorie, before a circle of eight opened up to admit them.

"Shall we?" Luke asked, eyeing the dance floor.

He didn't sound too enthusiastic and Rorie didn't blame him. "Would it be all right if we sat out the first couple of dances?" she asked. "I'd like to get more into the swing of things."

"No problem."

Luke looked almost grateful for the respite, which didn't lend Rorie much confidence. No doubt, he assumed this city slicker was going to make a fool of herself and him—and she probably would. When he escorted her to the row of chairs, Rorie made the mistake of sitting down. Instantly her skirts leapt up into her face. Embarrassed she pushed them down, then tucked the material under her thighs in an effort to tame the layers of stiff petticoats.

"Hello, Luke." A pretty blonde with sparkling blue eyes sauntered over. "I didn't know if you'd show tonight or not. Glad you did."

"Betty Hammond, this is Rorie Campbell."

Rorie nodded. "It's nice to meet you, Betty."

"Oh, I heard about you at the drugstore yesterday. You're the gal with the broken-down sports car, aren't you?"

"That's me." By now it shouldn't have surprised Rorie that everyone knew about her troubles.

"I hope everything turns out all right for you."

"Thanks." Although Betty was speaking to Rorie, her eyes didn't leave Luke. It was more than obvious that she expected an invitation to dance.

"Luke, why don't you dance with Betty," Rorie suggested, "That way I'll gather a few pointers from watching the two of you."

"What a good idea," Betty chirped eagerly. "We'll stay on the outskirts of the crowd so you can see how it's done. Be sure and listen to Charlie—he's the caller. That way you'll see what each step is."

Rorie nodded, agreeably.

Luke gave Rorie a long sober look. "You're sure?"

"Positive."

All join hands, circle right around
Stop in place at your hometown...

Studying the dancers, Rorie quickly picked up the terms *do se do*, *allemande left* and *allemande right* and a number of others, which she struggled to keep track of. By the end of the dance, her mind was buzzing. Her foot tapped out the lively beat of the fiddlers' music and a smile formed as she listened to the perfectly rhyming words.

"Rorie," Skip cried, suddenly standing in front of her. "May I have the pleasure of this dance?"

"I...I don't think I'm ready yet."

"Nonsense." Without listening to her protest, reached for her hand and hauled her to her feet.

"Skip, I'll embarrass you," she protested in a low whisper. "I've never done this before."

"You've got to start sometime." He tucked his arm around her waist and led her close to the stage.

"We got a newcomer, Charlie," Skip called out, "so make this one simple."

Charlie gave Skip a thumbs-up sign and reached for the microphone. "We'll go a bit slower this time," Charlie announced to his happy audience. "Miss Rorie Campbell from San Francisco has joined us and it's her first time on the floor."

Rorie wanted to curl up and die as a hundred faces turned to stare at her. But the dancers were shouting and cheering their welcome and Rorie shyly raised her hand, smiling into the crowd.

Getting through that first series of steps was the most difficult, but soon Rorie was in the middle, stepping and twirling—and laughing. Something she'd always assumed to be a silly, outdated activity turned out to be great fun.

By the time Skip led her back to her chair, she was breathless. "Want some punch?" he asked. Rorie nodded eagerly. Her throat felt parched.

When Skip left her, Luke Rivers appeared at her side. "You did just great," he said enthusiastically.

"For a city girl, you mean," she teased.

"As good as anyone," he insisted.

"Thanks."

"I suspect I owe you an apology, Rorie."

"Because you didn't want to make a fool of yourself with me on the dance floor?" she asked with a light laugh. "I don't blame you. Kate and Clay practically threw me in your lap. I'm sure you had other plans for tonight, and I'm sorry for your sake, that we got stuck with each other."

Luke grinned. "Trust me, I've had plenty of envious stares from around the room tonight. Any of a dozen different men would be more than happy to be 'stuck' with you.''

That went a long way toward boosting her ego. She would have commented, but Skip returned just then with a paper cup filled with bright pink punch. A teenage girl was beside him, clutching his free arm and smiling dreamily up at him.

''I'm going to dance with Caroline now, okay?'' he said to Rorie.

''That's fine,'' she answered smiling ''and thank you for braving the dance floor with me that first time.'' Skip blushed as he slipped an arm around Caroline's waist and hurried her off.

''You game?'' Luke nodded toward the dancing couples.

Rorie didn't hesitate. She swallowed the punch in three giant gulps, and gave him her hand. Together they moved onto the crowded floor.

By the end of the third set of dances, Rorie had twirled around with so many different partners, she lost track of them. She'd caught sight of Clay only once, and when he saw her, he waved. Returning the gesture, she promptly missed her footing and nearly fell into her partner's waiting arms. The tall sheriff's deputy was all too pleased to have her throw herself at him and told her as much, to Rorie's embarrassment.

Although it was only ten o'clock, Rorie was exhausted and so warm the perspiration ran in rivulets down her face and neck. She had to escape. Several times, she'd tried to sit out a dance, but no one would listen to her excuses.

In an effort to catch her breath and cool down, Rorie took advantage of a break between sets to wander outside. The night air was light and refreshing. Quite a few other people had apparently had the same idea, as the field that served as a parking lot was crowded with groups and strolling couples.

As she made her way through the dimly lit field, a handful of men who passing around a flask of whiskey and entertaining each other with off-color jokes. She steered a wide circle around them and headed toward Luke's parked car, deciding it was far enough away to discourage anyone from following her. In her eagerness to escape, she nearly stumbled over a couple locked in a passionate embrace against the side of a pickup.

Rorie mumbled an apology when the pair glanced up at her, irritation written all over their young faces. Good grief, she'd only wanted a few minutes alone in order to get a breath of fresh air—she hadn't expected to walk through an obstacle course!

When she finally arrived at Luke River's car, she leaned on the fender and slowly inhaled the clean country air. All her assumptions about this evening had been wrong. She'd been so sure she'd feel lonely and bored and out of place. And she'd felt none of those things. If she were to tell Dan about the Grange dance, he'd laugh at the idea of having such a grand time with a bunch of what he'd refer to as "country bumpkins." The thought irritated her briefly. These were good, friendly, fun-loving people. They'd taken her under their wing, expressed their welcome without reserve, and now they were showing her an uncomplicated lifestyle that had more appeal than Rorie would have thought possible.

"I thought I'd find you out here."

Rorie's whole body tensed as she recognized the voice of the man who had joined her.

"Hello, Clay."

CHAPTER EIGHT

RORIE FORCED a cheerful note into her voice. She turned around, half expecting Kate to be with him. The two had been inseparable from the minute Clay had arrived at the Logan house. It was just as well that Kate was around, since her presence prevented Clay and Rorie from giving in to any temptation.

Clay's hands settled on her shoulders and Rorie flinched involuntarily at his touch. With obvious regret and reluctance, Clay dropped his hands.

"Are you having a good time?" he asked.

She nodded enthusiastically. "I didn't think I would, which tells you how prejudiced I've been about country life, but I've been pleasantly surprised."

"I'm glad." His hands clenched briefly at his sides, then he flexed his fingers a couple of times. "I would have danced with you myself, but—"

She stopped him abruptly. "Clay, no. Don't explain . . . it isn't necessary. I understand."

His eyes held hers with such tenderness that she had to look away. The magical quality was back in the air— Rorie could feel it as forcefully as if the stars had spelled it out across the heavens.

"I don't think you do understand, Rorie," Clay said, "but it doesn't matter. You'll be gone in a couple of days and both our lives will go back to the way they were meant to be."

Rorie agreed with a quick nod of her head. It was too tempting, standing in the moonlight with Clay. Much too tempting. The memory of another night in which they'd stood and gazed at the stars returned with powerful intensity. Rorie realized that even talking to each other, alone like this, was dangerous.

"Won't Kate be looking for you?" she asked carefully.

"No. Luke Rivers is dancing with her."

For a moment she closed her eyes, not daring to look up at Clay. "I guess I'll be going inside now. I only came out to catch my breath and cool down a little."

"Dance with me first—here in the moonlight."

A protest surged within her, but the instant Clay slid his arms around her waist, Rorie felt herself give in. Kate would have him the rest of her life, but Rorie only had these few hours. Almost against her will, her hands found his shoulders, slipping around his neck with an ease that brought a sigh of pleasure to her lips. Being held by Clay shouldn't feel this good.

"Oh, Rorie," he moaned as she settled into his embrace.

They fit together as if they'd been created for one another. His chin touched the top of her head and he gently caressed her hair with his jaw.

"This is a mistake," Rorie murmured, closing her eyes, savoring the warm, secure feel of his arms.

"I know..."

But neither seemed willing to release the other.

His mouth found her temple and he kissed her there softly. "God help me, Rorie, what am I going to do? I haven't been able to stop thinking about you. I don't sleep, I hardly eat..." His voice was raw, almost savage.

"Oh, please," she said with a soft cry. "We can't . . . we mustn't even talk like this." His gray eyes smoldered above hers, and their breaths merged as his mouth hovered so close to her own.

"I vowed I wouldn't touch you again."

Rorie looked away. She'd made the same promise to herself. But it wasn't in her to deny him now, although her mind frantically searched for the words to convince him how wrong they were to risk hurting Kate— and each other.

His hands drifted up from her shoulders, his fingertips grazing the sides of her neck, trailing over her cheeks and through the softness of her hair. He placed his index finger over her lips, gently stroking them apart.

Rorie moaned. She moistened her lips with the tip of her tongue. Clay's left hand dug into her shoulders as her tongue caressed the length of his finger, drawing it into her mouth and sucking it gently. She needed him so much in that moment, she could have wept.

"Just this once . . . for these few minutes," he pleaded, "let me pretend you're mine." His hands cupped her face and slowly brought her mouth to his, smothering her whimper of part welcome, part protest.

A long series of kisses followed. Deep, relentless, searching kisses that sent her heart soaring. Kisses that only made the coming loneliness more painful. A sob swelled within her and tears burned her eyes as she twisted away and tore her mouth from his.

"No," she cried, covering her face with her hands and turning her back to him. "Please, Clay. We shouldn't be doing this."

He was silent for so long that Rorie suspected he'd left her. She inhaled a deep, calming breath and dropped her hands limply to her sides.

"It would be so easy to love you, Rorie."

"No," she whispered, shaking her head vigorously as she faced him again. "I'm not the right person for you—it's too late for that. You've got Kate." She couldn't keep the pain out of her voice. Anything between them was hopeless, futile. Within a day or two her car would be repaired and she'd vanish from his life as suddenly as she'd appeared.

Clay fell silent, his shoulders stiff and resolute as he stood silhouetted against the light of the Grange Hall. His face was masked by the shadows and Rorie couldn't read his thoughts. He drew in a harsh breath.

"You're right, Rorie. We can't allow this...attraction between us get out of hand. I promise you, by all I hold dear, that I won't kiss you again."

"I'll...do my part, too," she assured him, feeling better now that they'd made this agreement.

His hand reached for hers and clasped it warmly. "Come on, I'll walk you back to the hall. We're going to be all right. We'll do what we have to do."

Clay's tone told her he sincerely meant it. Relieved Rorie silently made the same promise to herself.

RORIE SLEPT LATE the following morning, later than she would have thought possible. Mary was busy with lunch preparations by the time she wandered down the stairs.

"Did you enjoy yourself last night?" Mary immediately asked.

In response, Rorie curtseyed and danced a few steps with an imaginary partner, clapping her hands.

Mary tried to hide a smile at Rorie's antics. "Oh, get away with you now. All I was looking for was a yes or a no."

"I had a great time."

"It was nothing like those city hotspots I'll wager."

"You're right about that," Rorie told her, pouring herself a cup of coffee.

"You seeing Kate today?"

Rorie shook her head and popped a piece of bread in the toaster. "She's got a doctor's appointment this morning and a teachers' meeting this afternoon. She's going to try to stop by later if she has a chance, but if not I'll be seeing her for sure tomorrow." Rorie intended to spend as much time as she could with Clay's fiancée. She genuinely enjoyed her company, and being with her served two useful purposes. It helped keep Rorie occupied, and it prevented her from being alone with Clay.

"What are you going to do today, then?" Mary asked, frowning.

Rorie laughed. "Don't worry. Whatever it is, I promise to stay out of your way."

The housekeeper gave a snort of amusement—or was it relief.

"Actually, I thought I'd type the data Clay needs for his pedigree-research program into the computer. There isn't much left and I should be able to finish by this afternoon."

"So if someone comes looking for you, that's where you'll be?"

"That's where I'll be," Rorie echoed. She didn't know who would "come looking for her," as Mary put it. The housekeeper made it sound as though a posse was due to arrive any minute demanding to know where the Franklin men were hiding Rorie Campbell.

Taking her coffee cup with her, Rorie walked across the yard and into the barn. Once more, she was impressed with all the activity that went on there. She'd come to know several of the men by their first names and returned their greetings with a smile and a wave.

As before, she found the office empty. She set down her cup while she turned on the computer and collected Clay's data. She'd just started to type it in when she heard someone enter the room. Pausing, she twisted her head around.

"Rorie."

"Clay."

They were awkward with one another now. Afraid, almost.

"I didn't realize you were here."

She stood abruptly. "I'll leave . . ."

"No. I came up to get something. I'll be gone in just a minute."

She nodded and sat back down. "Okay."

He walked briskly to his desk and sifted through the untidy stacks of papers. His gaze didn't waver from the task, but his jaw was tight, his teeth clenched. Impatience marked his every move. "Kate told me you're involved with a man in San Francisco. I . . . didn't know."

"I'm not exactly involved with him—at least not in the way you're implying. His name is Dan Rogers, and we've been seeing each other for about six months. He's divorced. The MG is his."

Clay's mouth thinned, but he still didn't look at her. "Are you in love with him?"

"No."

Lowering his head, Clay rubbed his hand over his eyes. "I had no right to ask you that. None. Forgive me, Rorie." Then clutching his papers, he stalked out of the office without a backward glance.

Rorie was so shaken by the encounter that when she went back to her typing, she made three mistakes in a row and had to stop to regain her composure.

When the phone rang, she ignored it, knowing Mary or one of the men would answer it. Soon afterward, she heard running footsteps behind her and swiveled around in the chair.

A breathless Skip bolted into the room. Shoulders heaving, he pointed in the direction of the telephone. "It's for you," he panted.

"Me?" It could only be Dan.

He nodded several times, his hand braced theatrically against his heart.

"Hello," she said, her fingers closing tightly around the receiver. "This is Rorie Campbell."

"Miss Campbell," came the unmistakable voice of George, the mechanic in Riversdale, "let me put it to you like this. I've got good news and bad news."

"Now what?" she cried, pushing her hair off her forehead with an impatient hand. She had to get out of Elk Run and the sooner the better.

"My man picked up the water pump for your car in Portland just the way we planned."

"Good."

George sighed heavily. "There's a minor problem, though."

"Minor?" She repeated hopefully.

"Well, not that minor actually."

"Oh, great . . . Listen, George, I'd prefer not to play guessing games with you. Just tell me what happened and how long it's going to be before I can get out of here.''

"I'm sorry, Miss Campbell, but they shipped the wrong part. It'll be two, possibly three days more.''

CHAPTER NINE

"WHAT'S WRONG?" Skip asked when Rorie indignantly replaced the telephone receiver.

She crossed her arms over her chest and breathed deeply, battling down the angry frustration that boiled inside her. The problem wasn't George's fault, or Skip's, or Kate's, or anyone else's.

"Rorie?" Skip asked again.

"They shipped the wrong part for the car," she returned flatly. "I'm going to be stuck here another two or possibly three days."

Skip didn't look the least bit perturbed at this bit of information. "Gee, Rorie, that's not so terrible. We like having you around—and you like it here, don't you?"

"Yes, but..." How could she explain that her reservations had nothing to do with their company, the stud farm or even with country life? She couldn't very well blurt out that she was falling in love with his brother, that she had to escape before she ruined their lives.

"But what?" Skip asked.

"My vacation."

"I know you had other plans, but you can relax and enjoy yourself here just as well, can't you?"

She didn't attempt to answer him, but closed her eyes and nodded, faintly.

"Well, listen, I've got to get back to work. Do you need me for anything?"

She shook her head. When the office door closed, Rorie sat back down in front of the computer again and poised her fingers over the keyboard. She sat like that unmoving, for several minutes as her thoughts churned. What was she going to do? Every time she came near Clay the attraction was so strong that trying to ignore it was like swimming upstream. Rorie had planned on leaving Elk Run the following day. Now she was trapped here for God only knew how much longer.

She got up suddenly and started pacing the office floor. Dan hadn't called her, either. She might have vanished from the face of the earth as far as he was concerned. The stupid car was his, after all, and the least he could do was make some effort to find out what had happened. Rorie knew she wasn't being entirely reasonable, but she was caught up in the momentum of her anger and frustration.

Impulsively she snatched the telephone receiver, had the operator charge the call to her San Francisco number and dialed Dan's office.

"Rorie, thank God you phoned," Dan said.

The worry in his voice appeased her a little. "The least you could have done was call me back," she fumed.

"I tried. My secretary apparently wrote down the wrong number. I've been waiting all this time for you to call back. Why didn't you? What on earth happened?"

She told him in detail, from the stalled car to her recent conversation with the mechanic. She didn't tell him about Clay Franklin and the way he made her feel.

"Rorie, baby, I'm so sorry."

She nodded mutely, close to tears. If she weren't so dangerously close to falling in love with Clay, none of this would seem such a disaster.

The silence lengthened while Dan apparently mulled things over. "Shall I come and get you?" he finally asked.

"With what?" she asked with surprising calm. "My car? You were the one who convinced me it would never make this trip. Besides, how would you get the MG back?"

"I'd find a way. Listen, baby, I can't let you sit around in some backwoods farm town. I'll borrow a car or rent one." He hesitated, then expelled his breath in a short burst of impatience. "Damn, forget that. I can't come."

"You can't?"

"I've got a meeting tomorrow afternoon. It's important—I can't miss it. I'm sorry, Rorie, I really am, but there's nothing I can do."

"Don't worry about it," she said, defeat causing her voice to dip slightly. "I understand." In a crazy kind of way she did. As a rising stockbroker, Dan's career moves were critical to him, more important than rescuing Rorie, the woman he claimed to love ... Somehow Rorie couldn't picture Clay making the same decision. In her heart she knew Clay would come for her the second she asked.

They spoke for a few minutes longer before Rorie ended the conversation. She felt trapped, as though the walls were closing in around her. So far she and Clay had managed to disguise their feelings, but they wouldn't be able to keep it up much longer before someone guessed. Kate wasn't blind, and neither was Mary.

"Rorie?" Clay called her name as he burst into the office. "What happened? Skip just told me you were all upset—something about the car? What's going on?"

"George phoned." She whirled around and pointed toward the telephone. "The water pump arrived just the way it was supposed to—but it's the wrong one."

Clay dropped his gaze, then removed his hat and wiped his forehead. "I'm sorry, Rorie."

"I am, too, but that doesn't do a bit of good, does it?" The conversation with Dan hadn't helped matters, and taking her frustration out on Clay wasn't going to change anything, either. "I'm stuck here, and this is the last place on earth I want to be."

"Do you think I like it any better?" he challenged.

Rorie blinked wildly at the tears that burned for release.

"I wish to God your car had broken down a hundred miles away from Elk Run," he said. "Before you bombarded your way into my home, my life was set. I knew what I wanted, where I was headed. In the course of a few days you've managed to uproot my whole world."

Emotion clogged Rorie's throat at the unfairness of his accusations. She hadn't asked for the MGB to break down where it had. The minute she could, she planned to get out of his life and back to her own.

No, she decided, they couldn't wait that long—it was much too painful for them both. She had to leave now. "I'll pack my things and be gone before evening."

"Just where do you plan to go?"

Rorie didn't know. "Somewhere . . . anywhere." She had to leave for his sake, as well as her own.

"Go back inside the house, Rorie, before I say or do something else I'll regret. You're right—we can't be in the same room together. At least not alone."

She started to walk past him, her eyes downcast, her heart heavy with misery. Unexpectedly his hand shot out and caught her fingers, stopping her.

"I didn't mean what I said." His voice rasped warm and hoarse. "None of it. Forgive me, Rorie."

Her heart raced when his hand touched hers. It took all the restraint Rorie could muster, which at the moment wasn't much, to resist wrapping herself in his arms and holding on for the rest of her life.

"Forgive me, too," she whispered.

"Forgive you?" he asked, incredulous. "No, Rorie. I'll thank God every day of my life for having met you." With that, he released her fingers, slowly, reluctantly. "Go now, before I make an even bigger fool of myself."

Rorie ran from the office as though a raging fire were licking at her heels, threatening to consume her.

And in a way, it was.

FOR TWO DAYS, Rorie managed to stay completely out of Clay's way. They saw each other only briefly and always in the company of others. Rorie was sure they gave Academy Award performances every time they were together. They laughed and teased and joked and the only one who seemed to suspect things weren't quite right was Mary.

Rorie was grateful the housekeeper didn't question her, but the looks she gave Rorie were frowningly thoughtful.

Three days after the Grange dance, Mary's sister arrived in Riversdale. Revealing more excitement than Rorie had seen in their brief acquaintance, Mary fussed with her hair and dress, and as soon as she finished the lunch dishes she was off.

Putting on Mary's well-worn apron, Rorie looped the long strands around her narrow waist twice and set to work. Kate joined her in midafternoon, carrying in a large bag of supplies for the dessert she was planning to prepare.

"I've been cooking from the moment Mary left," Rorie told Kate, pushing the damp hair from her forehead, as she stirred wine into a simmering sauce. Rorie intended to razzle-dazzle Clay and Skip with her one specialty—seafood fettuccine. She hadn't admitted to Mary how limited her repertoire of dishes was, although the housekeeper had repeatedly quizzed her about what she planned to make for dinner. Rorie had insisted it was a surprise. She'd decided that this rich and tasty dish stood a good chance of impressing the Franklin men.

"And I'm making Clay his favorite dessert—homemade lemon meringue pie." Kate reached for the grocery bag on the kitchen counter and six bright yellow lemons rolled onto the counter.

Rorie was impressed. The one and only time she'd tried to bake a lemon pie, she'd used a pudding mix. Apparently, Kate took the homemade part seriously.

"Whatever you're cooking smells wonderful," Kate said, stepping over to the stove. Fresh cracked crab, large succulent shrimp and small bite-sized pieces of sole were waiting in the refrigerator, to be added to the sauce just before the dish was served.

Kate was busy whipping up a pie crust when the phone rang several minutes later. She glanced anxiously at the wall, her fingers sticky with flour and lard.

Rorie looked over at her. "Do you suppose I should answer that?"

"You'd better. Clay usually relies on Mary to catch the phone for him."

Rorie lifted the receiver before the next peal. "Elk Run."

"That Miss Campbell?"

Rorie immediately recognized the voice of the mechanic from Riversdale. "Yes, this is Rorie Campbell."

"Remember I promised I'd call you when the part arrived? Well, it's here, all safe and sound, so you can stop fretting. It just came in a few minutes ago—haven't even had a chance to take it out of the box. Just thought you'd want to know."

"It's the right one this time?"

"Here I'll just check it now... Yup, this is it."

Rorie wasn't sure what she felt. Relief, yes, but regrets, too. "Thank you. Thank you very much."

"It's a little late for me to be starting the job this afternoon. My son's playing a little-league game and I told him I'd be there. I'll get to it first thing in the morning, and should be finished before noon. Just give me a call before you head out and I'll make sure everything's running the way it should be."

"Yes, I'll do that. Thanks again." Slowly Rorie replaced the telephone receiver. She leaned against the wall sighing deeply. At Kate's questioning gaze, she smiled weakly and explained, "That was the mechanic. The water pump for my car arrived and he's going to be working on it first thing in the morning."

"Rorie, that's great."

"I think so, too." She did—and she didn't. Part of her longed to flee Elk Run, and another part of her realized that no matter how far she traveled, no matter how many years passed, these days with Clay Franklin would always be special to her.

"Then tonight's going to be your last evening here," Kate murmured thoughtfully, looking disappointed. "Oh, dear, Rorie, as selfish as it sounds I really hate the thought of you leaving."

"We can keep in touch."

"Oh yes, I'd like that. I promise to send you a wedding invitation."

That reminder was the last thing Rorie needed. But once she was on the road again, she could start forgetting, she told herself grimly.

"Since this is going to be your last night, I think we should make it special," Kate announced brightly. "We're going to use the best china and set out the crystal wineglasses."

Rorie laughed, imagining Mary's face when she heard about it.

Even as she spoke, Kate was walking toward the dining-room china cabinet. In a matter of minutes, she'd set the table, cooked the sauce for the pie and poured it into the cooling pie shell that sat on the counter. The woman was a marvel!

Rorie was busy adding the final touches to the fettuccine when Clay and Skip came in through the back door.

"When's dinner?" Skip wanted to know. "I'm starved."

"In a few minutes." Rorie tested the boiling noodles to be sure they'd cooked all the way through but weren't overdone.

"Upstairs with the both of you," Kate said, shooing them out of the kitchen. "I want you to change into something nice."

"You want us to dress up for dinner?" Skip complained. He'd obviously recovered from any need to impress her with his sartorial elegance, Rorie noted, remembering that he'd worn his Sunday best that first night. "We already washed—what more do you want?"

"For you to change your clothes. We're having a celebration tonight."

"We are?" The boy's gaze slid from Kate to Rorie and then back again.

"That's right," Kate continued, undaunted by his lack of enthusiasm. "And when we're through with dinner, there's going to be a farewell party for Rorie. We're going to send her off country-style."

"Rorie's leaving?" Skip sounded as though that was the last thing he'd expected to hear. "But she just got here."

"The repair shop called from Riversdale. Her car will be finished tomorrow and she'll be on her way."

Clay's eyes burned into Rorie's. She tried to avoid looking at him, but when she did chance to meet his gaze, she could feel his distress. His jaw went rigid, and his mouth tightened as though he was bracing himself against Kate's words.

"Now hurry up, you two. Dinner's nearly ready," Kate said with a laugh. "Rorie's been cooking her heart out all afternoon."

Both men disappeared and Rorie set out the fresh green salad she'd made earlier, along with the seven grain dinner rolls she'd warmed in the oven.

Once everyone was seated at the table and waiting, Rorie ceremonially carried in the platter of fettuccine, thick with seafood. She'd spent a good ten minutes arranging it to look as attractive as possible.

"Whatever it is smells good," Skip called out as she entered the dining room. "I'm so hungry I could eat a horse."

"Funny, Skip, very funny," Kate said.

Rorie set the serving dish in the middle of the table and stepped back, anticipating their praise.

Skip raised himself halfway out of his seat as he glared at her masterpiece. "That's it?" His young voice was filled with disappointment.

Rorie blinked, uncertain how she should respond.

"You've been cooking all afternoon and you mean to tell me that's everything?"

"It's seafood fettuccine," she explained.

"It just looks like a bunch of noddles to me."

CHAPTER TEN

"I'LL HAVE ANOTHER PIECE of lemon pie," Skip said, eagerly extending his plate.

"If you're still hungry, Skip," Clay remarked casually, "there are a few dinner rolls left."

Skip's gaze darted to the small wicker basket and he wrinkled his nose. "No thanks, there're too many seeds in those things. I got one caught in my tooth earlier and spent five minutes trying to suck it out."

Rorie did her best to smile.

Skip must have noticed how miserable she was because he added, "the salad was real good though. What kind of dressing was that?"

"Vinaigrette."

"Really? It tasted fruity."

"It was raspberry flavored."

Skip's eyes widened. "I don't think I've ever heard of that kind of fancy vinegar. Did you buy it here in Nightingale?"

"Not exactly. I got the ingredients while Kate and I were out the other day and mixed it up last night."

"*That* tasted real good." Which was Skip's less-than-subtle method of telling her nothing else had. He'd barely touched the main course. Clay had made a show of asking for seconds, but Rorie was all too aware that his display of enthusiasm had been an effort to salve her injured ego.

Rorie wasn't fooled—no one had enjoyed her special dinner. Even old Blue had turned his nose up at it when she'd offered him a taste of the leftovers. The Labrador had covered his nose with a paw.

Clay and Skip did hard physical work; they didn't sit in an office all day like Dan and the other men she knew. She should have realized that Clay and his brother required a more substantial meal than noodles swimming in a creamy sauce. Rorie wished she'd discussed her menu with either Mary or Kate. A tiny voice inside her suggested that Kate might have said something to warn her. . . .

"Anyone else for more pie?" Kate was asking.

Clay nodded and cast a guilty glance in Rorie's direction. "I could go for a second piece myself."

"The pie was delicious," Rorie told Kate, meaning it. She was willing to admit Kate's dessert had been the highlight of the meal.

"Kate's one of the best cooks in the entire country," Skip announced, licking the back of his fork. "Her lemon pie won a blue ribbon at the county fair last year." He leaned forward, planting his elbows on the table. "She's got a barbecue sauce so tangy and good that when she cooks up spareribs I just can't stop eating 'em." His face fell as though he was thinking about those ribs now and would have gladly traded all of Rorie's fancy city food for a plateful.

"I'd like the recipe to the fettuccine if you'd give it to me," Kate told Rorie, obviously doing her best to change the subject and spare Rorie's feelings. Perhaps she felt a little guilty, too, for not giving her any helpful suggestions.

Skip stared at Kate as if she'd volunteered to muck out the stalls.

"I'll write it down before I leave."

"Since Rorie and Kate put so much time and effort into the meal, I think Skip and I could be convinced to do our part and wash the dishes."

"We could?" Skip protested.

"It's the least we can do," Clay returned flatly, glaring at his younger brother.

Rorie was all too aware of Clay's ploy. He wanted to get into the kitchen so they could find something else to eat without being obvious about it.

"Listen, you guys," Rorie said brightly. "I'm sorry about dinner. I can see everyone's still hungry. You're all going out of your way to reassure me, but it just isn't necessary."

"I don't know what you're talking about, Rorie. Dinner was excellent," Clay said, patting his stomach.

Rorie nearly laughed out loud. "You're starving and you know it. Why don't we call out for a pizza," she said, pleased with her solution. "I bungled dinner, so that's the least I can do to make it up to you."

Three faces stared at her blankly.

"Rorie," Clay said gently. "The closest pizza parlor is thirty miles from here."

"Oh."

Undeterred, Skip leapt to his feet. "No problem... You phone in the order and I'll go get it."

EMPTY PIZZA BOXES littered the living-room floor along with several abandoned pop cans.

Skip lay on his back staring up at the ceiling. "Anyone for a little music?" he asked lazily.

"Sure." Kate got to her feet and sat down at the piano. As her nimble fingers ran over the keyboard, the rich sounds echoed against the walls. "Anyone for a little Lee Greenwood?"

"All *right*," Skip called out with a holler, punching his fist into the air. He thrust two fingers in his mouth and gave a shrill whistle.

"Who?" Rorie asked once the commotion had died down.

"He's a country singer," Clay explained. Blue ambled to his side, settling down at his feet. Clay gently stroked his back.

"I guess I haven't heard of him," Rorie murmured. Once more she discovered three pairs of curious eyes studying her.

"What about Johnny Cash?" Kate suggested next. "You probably know who he is."

"Oh, sure." Rorie looped her arms over her bent knees and lowered her voice to a gravelly pitch. "I hear that train a comin'."

Skip let loose with another whistle and Rorie laughed at his boisterous antics. Clay left the room and returned a moment later with a guitar, then seated himself on the floor again, beside Blue. Skip crawled across the braided rug in the center of the room and retrieved a harmonica from the mantel. Soon Kate and the two men were making their own brand of music—country songs, from the traditional to the more recent. Rorie didn't know a single one, but she clapped her hands and tapped her foot to the lively beat.

"Sing for Rorie," Skip shouted to Clay and Kate. "Let's show her what she's been missing."

Clay's rich baritone joined Kate's lilting soprano, and Rorie's hands and feet stopped moving. Her eyes darted from one to the other in open-mouthed wonder at the beautiful harmony of their two voices, male and female. It was as though they'd been singing together all their lives. She realized maybe they had.

When they finished, Rorie blinked back tears, too dumbfounded for a moment to speak. "That was wonderful," she told them and her voice caught with emotion.

"Kate and Clay sing duets at church all the time," Skip explained. "They're good, aren't they?"

Rorie nodded, gazing at the two of them. She felt her heart might burst with the emotion that had welled up in her. Clay and Kate were right for each other—they belonged together, and once she was gone, they would blend their lives as beautifully as they had their voices. Rorie happened to catch Kate's eye. The other woman slipped her arms around Clay's waist and rested her head against his shoulder, laying claim to this man and silently letting Rorie know it. Rorie couldn't blame Kate. In like circumstances she would have done the same.

"Do you sing, Rorie?" Kate asked, leaving Clay and sliding onto the piano bench.

"A little, along with some piano." Actually her own singing voice wasn't half-bad. She'd participated in several singing groups while she was in high school and had taken five years of piano lessons.

"Please sing something for us." Rorie recognized a hint of challenge in the words.

"Okay." She replaced Kate at the piano bench and started out with a little satirical ditty she remembered from her college days. Skip hooted as she knew he would at the clever words, and all three rewarded her with a round of applause when she'd finished.

"Go ahead and play some more," Kate encouraged. "It's nice to have someone else do the playing for once." She sat next to Clay on the floor, resting her head against his shoulder. If it hadn't been for the guitar in his hands, Rorie knew he would have placed his arm over her shoulders and drawn her even closer. It would have been the natural thing to do.

"I don't think I know how to play the songs you usually sing, though." Rorie was more than a little reluctant now. She'd never heard of this Greenwood person they seemed to like so well.

"Play what you know," Kate said, "and we'll join in."

After a few seconds' thought, Rorie nodded. "This is a song by Billy Ocean. You might have heard of him—his songs are more rock than country, but I think you'll recognize the music." Rorie wasn't more than a few measures into the ballad before she realized that Kate, Clay and Skip had never heard of Billy Ocean.

She stopped playing. "What about Whitney Houston?"

Skip repeated the name a couple of times before his eyes lit up with recognition. "Hasn't she done Coke commercials?"

"Right," Rorie said, laughing. "She's had several big hits."

Kate slowly shook her head, looking discouraged. "Sorry, Rorie, I don't think I can remember the words to her songs."

"Barbra Streisand?"

"I thought she was an actress," Skip said with a puzzled frown. "You mean she sings, too?"

Reluctantly Rorie rose from the piano bench. "I'm sorry, Kate, you'll have to take over. It seems you three are a whole lot country and I'm a little bit rock and roll."

"We'll make you into a country girl yet!" Skip insisted, sliding the harmonica across his mouth with an ease Rorie envied.

Clay glanced at his watch. "We aren't going to be able to convert Rorie within the next twelve hours."

A gloom settled over them as Kate replaced Rorie at the piano.

"Are you sure we can't talk you into staying a few more days," Skip asked. "We're just starting to know each other."

Rorie shook her head, more determined than ever to leave as soon as she could.

"It would be a shame for you to miss the county fair next weekend—maybe you could stop here on your way back through Oregon, after your trip to Canada," Kate added. "Clay and I are singing, and we're scheduled for the square-dance competition, too."

"Yeah," Skip cried. "And we've got pig races planned again this year."

"Pig races?" Rorie echoed faintly.

"I know it sounds silly, but it's really fun. We take the ten fastest pigs in the area and let them race toward a bowl of Oreos. No joke—cookies! Everyone bets on who'll win and we all have a really good time." Skip's eyes shone with eagerness. "Please think about it, anyway, Rorie."

"Mary's entering her apple pie again," Clay put in. "She's been after that blue ribbon for six years."

A hundred reasons for Rorie to fade out of their lives flew across her mind like particles of dust in the wind. And yet the offer was tempting. She tried, unsuccessfully, to read Clay's eyes, her own filled with a silent appeal. This was a decision she needed help making. But Clay wasn't helping. The thought of never seeing him again was like pouring salt onto an open wound; still, it was a reality she'd have to face sooner or later.

So Rorie offered the only excuse she could come up with at the moment. "I don't have the time. I'm sorry, but I'd be cutting it too close to get back to San Francisco for work Monday morning."

"Not if you canceled part of your trip to Canada and came back on Friday," Skip pointed out, having given the matter some thought. "You didn't think you'd have a good time at the square dance, either, but you did, remember?"

It wasn't a matter of having a good time. So much more was involved . . . though the pig races actually sounded like fun. The very idea of such an activity would have astounded her only a week before, Rorie reflected. She could just imagine what Dan would say about it.

"Rorie?" Skip pressed. "What do you think?"

"I . . . I don't know."

"The county fair is about as good as it gets around Nightingale."

"I don't want to impose on your hospitality again." Clay still wasn't giving her any help with this decision.

"But having you stay with us isn't any problem," Skip insisted. "As long as you promise to stay out of the kitchen, you're welcome to stick around all summer. Isn't that right, Clay?"

His hesitation was so slight that Rorie doubted anyone else had noticed it. "Naturally Rorie's welcome to visit us any time she wants."

"If staying with these two drives you crazy," Kate inserted, "you could stay at my house. In fact, I'd love it if you did."

Rorie dropped her gaze, fearing what she might read in Clay's eyes. She sensed his indecision as she struggled with her own. She had to leave. Yet she wanted to stay...

"I think I should make what I can out of the rest of my vacation in Victoria," she finally told them.

"I know you're worried about getting back in time for work, but Skip's right. If you left Victoria one day early, then you could be here for the fair," Kate suggested again, but her offer didn't sound nearly as sincere as it had earlier.

"Rorie said she doesn't have the time," Clay said after an awkward silence. "I think we should all respect her decision."

"You sound like you don't want her to come back," Skip accused.

"No," Clay murmured, his gaze finding hers. "I want her here, but I think Rorie should try to salvage some of the vacation she planned. She has to do what she thinks best."

Rorie could feel his eyes moving over her hair and her face in loving appraisal. She tensed and prayed that Kate and Skip hadn't noticed.

During the next hour, Skip tried repeatedly to convince Rorie to visit on her way back or even to stay on until the fair. As far as Skip could see, there wasn't much reason to go to Canada now, anyway. But Rorie resisted. Walking away from Clay once was going to be painful enough. Rorie didn't know if she could do it twice.

Skip was yawning by the time they decided to call an end to the evening. With little more than a mumbled good night, he hurried up the stairs, abandoning the others.

Rorie and Kate took a few extra minutes to straighten the living room, while Clay drove the pickup around to the front of the house. "I think I'd better burn the evidence before Mary sees these pizza boxes," Rorie joked. "She'll have my hide once she hears about dinner."

Kate laughed good-naturedly as she collected her belongings. When they heard Clay's truck, she put down her bags and ran to Rorie. "You'll call me before you leave tomorrow?"

Rorie nodded and hugged her back.

"If something happens and you change your mind about the fair, please know that you're welcome to stay with me and Dad—we'd enjoy the company."

"Thank you, Kate."

The house felt empty and silent once Kate had left with Clay. Rorie knew it would be useless to go upstairs and try to sleep. Instead she wandered onto the front porch where she'd sat in the swing with Clay that first night. She sank down on the porch steps, one arm wrapped around a post, and gazed upward. The skies were alive with the glittering light of countless stars— stars that shone with a clarity and brightness one couldn't see in the city.

Clay belonged to this land, this farm, this small town. Rorie was a city girl to the marrow of her bones. This evening had proved the hopelessness of any dream that she and Clay might have of finding happiness together. There was his commitment to Kate. And there was the fact that he and Rorie were too different, their tastes too dissimilar. She certainly couldn't picture him making a life away from Elk Run.

Clay had accepted the hopelessness of it, too. That was the reason he'd insisted she travel to Canada. This evening Rorie had sensed a desperation in him that rivaled her own. It was a night filled with insights. Sitting under the heavens, she was beginning to understand some important things about life. For perhaps the first time, she'd fallen in love. The past six days she'd tried to deny what she was feeling, but on the eve of her departure, it seemed silly to lie to herself any longer. Rorie couldn't believe something like this had actually happened to her. Meeting someone and falling in love with him in the space of a few days was an experience reserved for novels and movies. This wasn't like her normal sane, sensible self at all. Rorie had always thought she was too levelheaded to fall so easily in love.

Until she met Clay Franklin.

On the wings of one soul-searching realization came another. Love wasn't what she'd anticipated. She'd assumed it meant a strong sensual passion that overwhelmed the lovers and left them powerless before it. But in the past few days, she'd learned that love marked the soul as well as the body.

Clay would forever be a part of her. Since that first night when Nightsong was born her heart had never felt more alive. Yet within a few hours she would walk away from the man she loved and consider herself blessed to have shared these days with him.

A tear rolled down the side of her face, surprising her. This wasn't a time for sadness, but joy. She'd discovered a deep inner strength she hadn't known she possessed. She wiped the moisture away and rested her head against the post, her gaze fixed on the heavens.

The footsteps behind Rorie didn't startle her. She'd known Clay would come to her this one last time.

CHAPTER ELEVEN

CLAY DRAPED HIS ARM over Rorie's shoulders and joined her in gazing up at the sky. Neither spoke for several moments, as though they feared words would destroy the tranquil mood. Rorie stared, transfixed by the glittering display. Like her love for this man, the stars would remain forever distant, unattainable, but certain and unchanging.

A ragged sigh escaped her lips. "All my life I've believed that everything that befalls us has a purpose."

"I've always thought that, too," Clay whispered.

"Everything in life is deliberate."

"Our final hours together you're going to become philosophical?" He rested his chin on the crown of her head, gently mussing her hair. "Are you sad, Rorie?"

"Oh, no," she denied quickly. "I can't be... I feel strange, but I don't know if I can find the words to explain it. I'm leaving tomorrow and I realize we'll probably never see each other again. I have no regrets—not a single one—and yet I think my heart is breaking."

His hand tightened on her shoulder in silent protest as if he found the thought of relinquishing her more than he could bear.

"We can't deny reality," she told him. "Nothing's going to change in the next few hours. The water pump on the car will be replaced, and I'll go back to my life. The way you'll go back to yours."

"I have this gut feeling there's going to be a hole the size of Grand Canyon in mine the minute you drive away." He dropped his arm and reluctantly moved away from her. His eyes held a weary sadness, but Rorie found an acceptance there, too.

"I'm an uncomplicated man," he stated evenly. "I'm probably nothing like the sophisticated man you're dating in San Francisco."

Her thoughts flew to Dan, so cosmopolitan and... superficial, and she recognized the truth in Clay's words. The two men were poles apart. Dan's interests revolved around his career and his car, but he was genuinely kind, and it was that quality that had attracted Rorie to him.

"Elk Run's given me a good deal of satisfaction over the years. My life's work is here and, God willing, some day my son will carry on the breeding programs I've started. Everything I've ever dreamed of has always been within my hand's grasp." He paused, holding in a long sigh, then releasing it slowly. "And then you came," he whispered, and a brief smile crossed his lips, "and within a matter of days, I'm reeling from the effects. Suddenly I'm left doubting what really is important in my life."

Rorie lowered her eyes. "Who would have believed a silly water pump would be responsible for all this wretched soul-searching?"

"I've always been the type of man who's known what he wants, but you make me feel like a schoolboy no older than Skip. I don't know what to do anymore, Rorie. Within a few hours, you'll be leaving and part of me says if you do, I'll regret it the rest of my life."

"I can't stay." Their little dinner party had shown her how different their worlds actually were. She wouldn't fit into his life and he'd be an alien in hers. But Kate...Kate belonged to his world.

Clay rubbed his hands across his eyes and harshly drew in a breath. "I know you feel you should leave, but that doesn't mean I have to like it."

"The pull to stay is there for me, too," she whispered.

"And it's tearing both of us apart."

Rorie shook her head. "Don't you see? So much good has come out of meeting you, Clay." Her voice was strong. She had to make him realize that she'd always be grateful for the things he'd taught her. "In some ways I became a woman tonight. I feel I'm doing what's right for both of us, though it's more painful than anything I've ever known."

He looked at her with such undisguised love that she ached all the way to the core of her being.

"Let me hold you once more," he said softly. "Give me that, at least."

Rorie sadly shook her head. "I can't... I'm so sorry, Clay, but this is how it has to be with us. I'm so weak where you're concerned. I couldn't bear to let you touch me now and then leave tomorrow."

His eyes drifted shut as he yielded to her wisdom. "I don't know that I could, either."

They were no more than a few feet apart, but it seemed vast worlds stood between them.

"More than anything I want you to remember me fondly, without any bitterness," Rorie told him, discovering as she spoke the words how much she meant them.

Clay nodded. "Be happy, Rorie, for my sake."

Rorie realized that contentment would be a long time coming without this man in her life, but she would find it eventually. She prayed that he'd marry Kate some-day, the way he'd planned. The other woman was the perfect wife for him—unlike herself. A thread of agony twisted around Rorie's heart.

She turned to leave him, fearing she'd dissolve into tears if she remained much longer. "Goodbye, Clay."

"Goodbye, Rorie."

She rushed past him and hurried up the stairs.

THE FOLLOWING MORNING, both Clay and Skip had left the house by the time Rorie entered the kitchen.

"Good morning, Mary," she said, forcing a note of cheerfulness in her voice. "How did the visit with your sister go?"

"Fine."

Rorie stepped around the housekeeper to reach the coffeepot and poured herself a cup. A plume of steam rose enticingly to her nostrils and she took a tentative sip, not wanting to burn her lips.

"I found those pizza boxes you were trying so hard to hide from me," Mary grumbled as she wiped her hands on her apron. "You fed these good men restaurant pizza?"

Unable to stop herself, Rorie chuckled at the house-keeper's indignation. "Guilty as charged. Mary, you should have known better than to leave their fate in my evil hands."

"Near as I can figure, the closest pizza parlor is a half hour or more away. Did you drive over and get it your-self or did you send Skip?"

"Actually he volunteered," she admitted reluc-tantly. "Dinner didn't exactly turn out the way I'd hoped."

The housekeeper snickered. "I should have known as much. You city slickers don't know nothing about serving up a decent meal to your menfolk."

Rorie gave a hefty sigh of agreement. "The only thing for me to do is stay on another month or two and have you teach me." As she expected, the housekeeper opened her mouth to protest. "Unfortunately," Rorie continued, cutting Mary off before she could launch into her arguments, "I'm hoping to be gone by afternoon."

Mary's response was a surprise. The older woman turned to face Rorie, and her eyes narrowed, intense and troubled.

"I suspected you'd be going soon enough," she said in a tight voice, pulling out a chair. She sat down heavily and her hand brushed wisps of gray hair from her forehead. Her weathered face grew more and more thoughtful. "It's for the best, you know."

"I knew you'd be glad to be rid of me."

Mary shrugged. "It's other reasons that make your leaving right. You know what I'm talking about, even if you don't want to admit it to me. As a person you tend to grow on folks. Like I said before, for a city girl, you ain't half-bad."

Rorie reached for a banana from the fruit bowl in the center of the table. She waved it like a baton, trying to lighten the mood, which had taken an unexpected turn toward the serious. "For a stud farm, stuck out here in the middle of nowhere, this place isn't half-bad, either. The people are friendly and the apple pie's been exceptional."

Mary ignored the compliment on her pie. "By people, I suppose you're referring to Clay. You're going to miss him, aren't you, girl?"

The banana found its way back into the bowl and, with it, the cheerful facade. "Yes. I'll miss Clay."

The older woman's frown deepened. "From the things I've been noticing, he's going to be yearning for you, as well. But it's for the best," she said quietly. "For the best."

Rorie nodded and her voice wavered. "Yes, I know...but it isn't easy."

The housekeeper gave her a lopsided smile as she gently patted Rorie's hand. "I know that, too, but you're doing the right thing. You'll forget him soon enough."

A strong protest rose in her breast, closing off her throat. She wouldn't forget Clay. Ever. How could she forget the man who had so unselfishly taught her such valuable lessons about life and love? Lessons about herself.

"Kate Logan's the right woman for Clay," Mary said abruptly.

Those few words cut Rorie to the quick. It was something she already knew, but hearing another person voice it made the truth almost unbearably painful.

"I...hope they're very happy."

"Kate loves him. She has from the time she was knee-high to a June bug. And there's something you don't know. Several years back, when Clay was in college, he fell in love with a girl from Seattle. She'd been born and raised in the city. Clay loved her, wanted to marry her, even brought her to Elk Run to meet the family. She stayed a couple of days, and the whole time, she was as restless as water on a hot skillet. Apparently she had words with Clay because the next thing I knew, she'd packed her bags and headed home. Clay never said much about her after that, but she hurt him bad. It wasn't until Kate was home from college that Clay thought seriously about marriage again.''

Mary's story explained a good deal about Clay.

"Now, I know I'm just an old woman who likes her soaps and Saturday-night bingo. Most folks don't think I've got a lick of sense, and that's all right. What others choose to assume don't bother me much.'' She paused, and shook her head. "But Kate Logan's about the kindest, dearest person this town has ever seen. People like her—can't help themselves. She's always got a kind word and there's no one in this world she's too good for. She cares about the people in this community. Those kids she teaches over at the grade school love her like nothing you've ever seen. And she loves them. When it came to building that fancy library, it was Kate who worked so hard convincing folks they'd be doing what was best for Nightingale by voting for that bond issue.''

Rorie kept her face averted. She didn't need Mary to tell her Kate was a good person; she'd seen the evidence of it herself.

"What most folks don't know is that Kate has seen plenty of pain in her own life. She watched her mother die a slow death from cancer. Took care of her most of the time herself, nursing Nora when she should have been off at college having fun like other nineteen-year-olds. Her family needed her and she was there. Kate gave old man Logan a reason to go on living when Nora passed away. She lives with him still, and it's long past time for her to be a carefree adult on her own. Kate's a good person clean through.'' Mary hesitated, then drew in a solemn breath. "Now, you may think I'm nothing but a meddling old fool, and I suspect you're right. But I'm saying it's a good thing you're leaving Elk Run before you break that girl's heart. She's got a chance now for some happiness, and God knows she deserves it. If she loses Clay, I know for certain it'd break her heart. She's too good to have that happen to her over some fancy city girl who's only passing through."

Rorie winced at the way Mary described her.

"I'm a plain talker," Mary said on the end of an abrupt laugh. "Always have been, always will be. Knowing Clay—and I do, as well as his mother did, God rest her soul—he'll pine for you awhile, but eventually everything will fall back into place. The way it was before you arrived."

Tears stung Rorie's eyes. She felt miserable as it was, and Mary wasn't helping any. She'd already assured the housekeeper she was leaving, but Mary apparently wanted to be damn certain she didn't change her mind and return. The woman didn't understand . . . but then again, maybe she did.

"Have you ever been in love, Mary?"

"Once," came the curt reply. "Hurt so much the first time I never chanced it again."

"Are you sorry you lived your life alone now?" That was what Rorie saw for herself. Oh, she knew she was being melodramatic and over-emotional, but she couldn't imagine loving any man as much as she did Clay.

Mary lifted one shoulder in a shrug. "Some days I have plenty of regrets, but then on others it ain't so bad. I'd like to have had a child, but God saw to it that I was around when Clay and Skip needed someone . . . Knowing that made up for what I missed."

"They consider you family."

"Yeah, I suppose they do." Mary pushed out her chair and stood up. "Well, I better get back to work.

Those men expect a good lunch. I imagine they're near starved after the dinner you fed them last night.''

Despite her heartache, Rorie smiled and drained the last of her coffee. ''And I'd better get upstairs and pack the rest of my things. The mechanic said my car would be ready around noon.''

On her way to the bedroom. Rorie paused at the framed photograph of Clay's parents that sat on the piano. She'd passed it several times and had given it little more than a fleeting glance. Now it suddenly demanded her attention, and she stopped in front of it.

A tremor went through her hand as she lightly ran her finger along the brass frame. Clay's mother smiled serenely into the camera, her gray eyes so like her son's that Rorie felt a knot twist in her stomach. Those same eyes seemed to reach across eternity and call out to Rorie, plead with her. Rorie's own eyes narrowed, certain her imagination was playing havoc with her troubled mind. She focused her attention on the woman's hair. That, too, was the same dark shade as Clay's, brushed away from her face in a carefully styled chignon. Clay had never mentioned his parents to her, not once, but just looking at the photograph, Rorie knew intuitively that he'd shared a close relationship with his mother. Blue wandered out from the kitchen and stood at Rorie's side as though offering consolation. Grateful, she reached down to pet him.

Looking back at the photograph, Rorie noted that Skip resembled his father, with the same dancing blue eyes that revealed more than a hint of devilry.

Rorie continued to study both parents, but it was Clay's mother who captured her attention over and over again.

The phone ringing in the distance startled her, and her wrist was shaking when she set the picture back on the piano.

"Phone's for you," Mary shouted from the kitchen.

Rorie already knew it was George at the repair shop in Riversdale; she'd been waiting all morning to hear from him.

"Hello," she said, her fingers closing tightly around the receiver. Her biggest fear was that something had happened to delay her departure a second time.

"Miss Campbell," said the mechanic, "everything's fine. I got that part in and working for you without a hitch."

"Thank God," she murmured. Her hold on the telephone receiver relaxed, a little.

"I've got a man I could spare if you'd like to have your car delivered to Elk Run. But you've got to understand fifty miles is a fair distance and I'm afraid I'll have to charge you extra for it."

"That's fine," Rorie said eagerly, not even bothering to ask the amount. "How soon can he be here?"

CHAPTER TWELVE

"So you're really going," Skip said as he picked up Rorie's bags. "Somehow I thought I might have talked you into staying on for the county fair."

"You seem intent on bringing me to ruin, Skip Franklin. I'm afraid I'd bet all my hard-earned cash on those pig races you were telling me about," Rorie teased. Standing in the middle of the master bedroom, she surveyed it one last time to be certain she hadn't forgotten anything.

A pang of wistfulness settled over her as she slowly looked around. Not for the first time, Rorie felt the love and warmth emanating from these brightly papered walls. Lazily, almost lovingly, she ran her fingertips along the top of the dresser, letting her hand linger there a moment, unwilling to pull herself away. This bedroom represented so much of what she was leaving behind. It was difficult to walk away.

Skip stood in the doorway impatiently waiting for her. "Kate phoned and said she's on her way over. She wants to say goodbye."

"I'll be happy to see her one last time." Rorie wished Skip would leave so she could delay her parting with this room a little longer. Until now, Rorie hadn't realized how much sleeping in Clay's parents' room had meant to her. Her appreciation had come too late.

"Mary's packing a lunch for you to take," Skip announced with a wry chuckle, "and knowing Mary, it'll be enough to last you a week."

Rorie smiled and reluctantly followed him down the stairs. As Skip had claimed, the housekeeper had prepared two large sacks, which sat waiting on the kitchen table.

"Might as well take those with you, too," Mary muttered gruffly. "I hate the thought of you eating restaurant food. This, at least, will stick to your ribs."

"Goodbye, Mary," Rorie said softly, touched by the housekeeper's thoughtfulness. On impulse she gently hugged the older woman. "Thank you for everything—including our talk this morning." The impromptu embrace surprised Rorie as much as it obviously did Mary.

"You drive careful now, you hear?" the housekeeper answered, squeezing Rorie tightly and patting her back several times.

"I will, I promise."

"A letter now and again wouldn't be amiss."

"All right," Rorie agreed, and rubbed the moisture from the corners of her eyes. These people had touched her in so many ways. Leaving them was far more difficult than she'd imagined.

The housekeeper rubbed the heel of her hand over her right eye. "It's time for you to get on the road. What are you doing standing in the kitchen chitchatting with me?" she asked brusquely.

"I'm going, I'm going." Mary's gruff voice didn't fool Rorie. The housekeeper's exterior might be a little crusty, and her tongue a bit surly, but she didn't succeed in disguising a generous, loving heart.

"I don't know where Clay is," Skip complained after he'd loaded the luggage into the MG's trunk. "I thought for sure he'd want to see you before you left. I wonder where he got off to."

"I'm ... sure he's got better things to do than say goodbye to me."

"Nothing is more important than this," Skip countered, frowning "I'm going to see if I can find him."

Rorie's first reaction was to stop Skip, then she quickly decided against it. If she made too much of a fuss, Skip might suspect something. She understood what had prompted Clay to stay away from the house all morning, and in truth, she was grateful. Leaving Elk Run was hard enough without prolonging the agony in lengthy farewells to Clay.

Skip hesitated, kicking at the dirt with the pointed toe of his cowboy boot. "You two didn't happen to have a fight or anything, did you?"

"No. What makes you ask?"

Skip shrugged. "I don't know ... It's just that every time I walked into a room with the two of you, I could feel something. If it wasn't for Kate, I'd think my big brother was sweet on you."

"I'm sure you're imagining things."

"I suppose so," Skip said with a curt nod, quickly dismissing the notion. "Ever since you arrived, though, Clay's been acting weird."

"How do you mean?"

"Sort of cranky."

"My unexpected arrival added to his troubles, don't you think?" In so many ways it was the truth, and she felt guilty about that. The responsibilities for the farm and for raising Skip were sobering enough; he didn't need her there to wreak havoc with his personal life.

"You weren't any problem," Skip answered sharply. "In fact, having you around was a lot of fun. The only trouble is you didn't stay near long enough."

"Thank you, Skip," she managed. Once again she felt her throat clog with tears. She was touched by his sweet, simple hospitality and reminded of how much she would miss him.

"I still kinda wish you were going to stay for the fair," he mumbled. "You'd have a good time, I guarantee it. We may not have all the fancy entertainment you do in San Francisco, but when we do something like a country fair, we do it big."

"I'm sure it'll be great fun."

Skip braced his foot against the bumper of the faded blue pickup, apparently forgetting his earlier decision to seek out Clay, which was just as well.

"You don't like the country much, do you, Rorie?"

"Oh, but I do," she countered. "It's a different way of life, though. I feel like a duck in a pond full of swans here on Elk Run."

Skip laughed. "I suppose folks there in the big city don't think much of the country."

"No one has time to think," Rorie said with a small laugh.

"That doesn't make any sense. Everyone's got thoughts."

Rorie nodded, not knowing how to explain something so complex. When Skip had spent some time in the city, he'd figure out what she meant.

"The one thing I've noticed more than anything is how quiet it is here," she said pensively, looking around, burning into her memory each detail of the farmhouse and the yard.

"I like the quiet. Some places, the noise is so bad I worry about ear damage," Skip said.

"I imagine if I were to live here, I'd grow accustomed to the silence, too. I hadn't ever thought about how much I enjoy the sounds of the city. There's something invigorating about the clang of the trolley cars or the foghorn on the Bay early in the morning."

Skip frowned and shook his head. "You honestly like all that racket?"

Rorie nodded. "It's more than that. There's something sensual about the city, exciting. I hadn't even realized how much living there meant to me before coming to Elk Run." Rorie didn't know how to describe the aroma of freshly baked sourdough bread, or the perfumed scent of budding rosebushes in the Golden Gate Park, to someone who had never experienced them. Country life had its appeal, she couldn't deny that, but she belonged to the city. At least, that was what she told herself over and over again.

"Ah," Skip said, and his foot dropped from the bumper with a thud, "here's Clay now."

Rorie tensed, gripping her hands together in front of her. Clay's lengthy strides quickly diminished the distance between the barn and the yard. Each stride was filled with purpose, as though he longed to get this polite farewell over with.

Rorie straightened and walked toward him. "I'll be leaving in a couple of minutes," she explained softly.

"Kate's coming over to say goodbye," Skip added.

Rorie noted how Clay's eyes didn't quite meet her own. He seemed to focus instead on the car behind her. They'd already said everything there was to say and this final parting only compounded the pain.

"Saying thank-you seems so inadequate," Rorie told him in a voice that wasn't entirely steady. "I've appreciated your hospitality more than you'll ever know." Hesitantly she held out her hand to him.

Clay's hard fingers curled around her own, his touch light and impersonal. Rorie swallowed hard, unable to hold back the emotion churning so violently inside her.

His expression was completely impassive, she noted, but she sensed that he held on to his self-control with the thinnest of threads. In that moment, Rorie felt the desperate longing in him and knew that he recognized it in her, too.

"Oh, Clay..." she whispered, her eyes brimming with tears. The impulse to move into his arms was like a huge wave, threatening to sweep over her, and she didn't know how much longer she'd have the strength to resist.

"Don't look at me like that," Clay muttered grimly.

"I...can't help it." But he belonged to Kate and nothing was likely to change that.

He took a step toward her and stopped himself, suddenly remembering they weren't alone.

"Skip, go hold Thunder for Don. Don's trying to paste-worm him, and he's getting dragged all over the stall." Clay's words were low-pitched, sharp, full of demand.

"But, Clay, Rorie's about to—"

"Do it."

Mumbling something unintelligible under his breath, Skip trudged off to the barn.

The minute his brother was out of sight, Clay caught Rorie's shoulders, his fingers felt rough and urgent through the thin cotton of her blouse. The next instant, she was locked against him. The kiss was inevitable, Rorie knew, but when his mouth settled over hers she wanted to weep for the joy she found in his arms. He kissed her temple, her cheek, her mouth, until she clung to him with hungry abandonment. They were standing in the middle of the yard in full view of farmhands, but Clay didn't seem to care and Rorie wasn't about object.

"I told myself I wouldn't do this," he whispered huskily.

Rorie's heart constricted.

At the sound of a car in the distance, Clay abruptly dropped his arms, freeing her. His fingers tangled in her hair as if he had to touch her one last time.

"I was a fool to think I could politely shake your hand and let you drive away from me. We're more than casual friends and I can't pretend otherwise—to hell with the consequences."

Tears flooded Rorie's eyes as she stared up at Clay. Then from behind him, she saw the cloud of dust that announced Kate's arrival. She inhaled a deep breath in an effort to compose herself and, wiping her damp cheeks with the back of one hand, forced a smile.

Clay released a ragged sigh as he trailed a callused hand down the side of her face. "Goodbye, Rorie," he whispered. With that, he turned and walked away.

A THICK LAYER OF FOG swirled around Rorie as she paused to catch her breath on the path in Golden Gate Park. She bent forward and planted her hands on her knees, driving the oxygen into her heaving lungs. Not once in the two weeks she'd been vacationing had she followed her jogging routine, and now she was paying the penalty. The muscles in her calves and thighs protested the strenuous exercise and her heart seemed about to explode. Her biggest problem was trying to keep up with Dan, who'd run ahead, unwilling to slow his pace to match hers.

"Rorie?"

"Over here." Her voice was barely more than a choked whisper. She meant to raise her hand and signal to him, but even that required more effort than she could manage. Seeing a bench in the distance, she stumbled over and collapsed into it. Leaning back, she stretched her legs in front of her.

"You *are* out of shape," Dan teased, handing her a small towel.

Rorie wiped the perspiration from her face and smiled her appreciation. "I can't believe two weeks would make such a difference." She'd been back in San Francisco only a couple of days. Other than dropping off the MG at Dan's place, this was the first time they'd had a chance to get together.

Dan sat down next to her, hardly out of breath. Even after a three-mile workout, he didn't have a hair out of place.

"Two weeks *is* a long time," he said with the hint of a smile. "I suppose you didn't keep up with your vitamin program, either," he chastised gently. "Well, Rorie, it's obvious how much you need me."

She chose to ignore that comment. "I used to consider myself in top physical condition. I ranked right up there with Jane Fonda and the rest of them. Not anymore. Good grief, I thought my heart was going to give out two miles back."

Dan, blond and debonair, was appealingly handsome in a clean-cut boyish way. He draped the towel around his neck and grasped the ends. Rorie's eyes were drawn to his hands, with their finely manicured nails and long tapered fingers. Stockbroker fingers. Nice hands. Friendly hands.

Still, Rorie couldn't help comparing them with another pair of male hands, darkly tanned from hours in the sun and roughly callused. Gentle hands. Working hands.

"I meant what I said about you needing me," Dan murmured, watching her closely. "It's time we got serious, Rorie. Time we made some important decisions about our future."

When she least expected it, he dropped onto the bench beside her. With his so smooth fingers, he cupped her face, his thumbs stroking her flushed cheeks. "I had time to do a lot of thinking while you were away."

She covered his fingers with her own, praying for an easier way to say what she must. They'd been seeing each other for months and she hated to hurt him, but it would be even crueller to lead him on. When they'd first started dating, Dan had been looking for a casual relationship. He'd recently been divorced and wasn't ready for a new emotional commitment.

"Oh, Dan, I think I know what you're going to say. Please don't."

He paused, searching her face intently. "What do you mean?"

"I had time to think while I was away, too, and I realized that although I'll always treasure your friendship, we can't ever be more than friends."

His dark eyes ignited with resistance. "What happened to you on this vacation, Rorie? You left, and two weeks later you returned a completely different woman."

"I'm sure you're exaggerating," Rorie objected weakly. She knew she *was* different, from the inside out.

"You've hardly said a word to me about your trip," Dan complained, in a tone that suggested he felt hurt by her reticence. "All you've said is that the car broke down in the Oregon outback and you were stuck there for days until a part could be delivered. You don't blame me for that, do you? I had no idea there was anything wrong with the water pump."

She laughed at his apt description of Nightingale as the outback.

"You completely missed the writers' conference, didn't you?"

"That couldn't be helped, but I enjoyed the rest of my vacation. Victoria was like stepping into a small piece of England," she said, in an effort to divert his attention from the time she'd spent on the Franklin farm. Victoria had been lovely, but unfortunately, she hadn't been in the proper mood to appreciate its special brand of beauty.

"You didn't so much as mail me a postcard."

"I know," she said with a twinge of guilt.

"I was lonesome without you," Dan said slowly, running his hand over her hair. "Nothing felt right with you gone."

Rorie realized it had taken a good deal for him to admit that, and it made what she had to tell him all the more difficult.

"Dan, please," she said, breaking away from him and standing. "I...I don't love you."

"But we're friends."

"Of course."

He seemed both pleased and relieved by that. "Good friends?" he coaxed.

Rorie nodded, wondering where this discussion was leading.

"Then there's really no problem, is there?" he asked, his voice gaining enthusiasm. "You went away, and I realized how much I love you, and you came back deciding you value my friendship—that, at least, is a beginning."

"Dan, honestly!"

"Well, isn't it?"

"Our relationship isn't going anywhere," she told him, desperate to clarify the issue. Dan was a good person and he deserved someone who was crazy in love with him. The way she was with Clay. Only Clay.

To Rorie's surprise, Dan drew her forward and soundly kissed her. Startled, she stood placidly in his arms, feeling his warm mouth move over hers. She experienced no feeling, no excitement, nothing. Kissing Dan held all the appeal of drinking flat soda.

Frustrated, he tried to deepen the kiss.

Rorie braced her hands against his chest and twisted her mouth free from him. He released her immediately, then stepped back, frowning. "Okay, okay, we've got our work cut out for us. But the electricity will come, in time."

Somehow Rorie doubted that.

Dan dropped her off in front of her apartment. "Can I see you soon?" he asked, his hands clenching the steering wheel. He didn't look at her but stared straight ahead as though he feared her answer.

Rorie hesitated. "I'm not going to fall in love with you, Dan, and I don't want to take advantage of your feelings. I think it'd be best if you started seeing someone else."

He appeared to mull that over for several awkward moments. "But the decision should be my own, don't you think?"

"Yes, but—"

"Then leave everything to me, and stop worrying. If I choose to waste my time on you, that's my problem, not yours. Personally I think you're going to change your mind. You see, Rorie, I love you enough for both of us."

"Oh, Dan." Her shoulders sagged with defeat. He hadn't believed a single word she'd said.

"Now stop looking so depressed. How about a movie Sunday? It's been a while since we've done that."

Exhausted, she shook her head. "Dan, no."

"I insist, so stop arguing."

She didn't have the energy to argue. Soon enough he'd learn she meant what she'd said. "All right."

"Good. I'll pick you up at six."

Rorie climbed out of the sedan and closed the door, turning to give Dan a limp wave. She paused in the foyer of her apartment building to unlock her mailbox.

There was a handful of envelopes. Absently, she shuffled through a flyer from a prominent department store, an envelope with a Kentucky postmark and an electric bill. It wasn't until she was inside her apartment that Rorie noticed the letter postmarked Nightingale, Oregon.

CHAPTER THIRTEEN

RORIE SET THE LETTER on her kitchen counter and
stared at it for several breathless moments. Her chest
felt as if a dead weight were pressing against it. Her
heart was pounding and her stomach churned. The
post-office box number for the return address didn't tell
her much. The letter could as easily be from Kate as
Clay. It could even be from Mary.

Taking a deep, calming breath, Rorie reached for the
envelope from Kentucky first. The return address left
her blank—she didn't know anyone who lived in that
state.

That single slip of paper inside confused her, too. She
read it several times, not understanding. It appeared to
be registration papers for Nightsong, from the National
Show Horse Association. Rorie Campbell was listed as
owner, with Clay's name given as breeder. The date of
Nightsong's birth was also recorded. Rorie slumped into
a kitchen chair and battled an attack of memories and
tears.

Clay was giving her Nightsong.

It was Nightsong who had brought them together and
it was by Nightsong that they would remain linked. Life
would go on; the loss of one woman's love wouldn't al-
ter the course of history. But now there was something—a single piece of paper—that would connect her

to Clay, something that gave testimony to their sacrifice.

Rorie had needed that and Clay had apparently known it.

They'd made the right decision, Rorie told herself for the hundredth time. Clay's action confirmed it.

Clay was wide-open spaces and sleek, well-trained horses, while she thrived in the crowded city.

His strength came from his devotion to the land; hers came from the love of children and literature and the desire to create her own stories.

They were dissimilar in every way—and alike. In the most important matters, the most telling, they were actually very much alike. Neither of them was willing to claim happiness at the expense of someone else.

Tears spilled down her cheeks, and sniffling, Rorie wiped them aside. The drops dampened her fingertips as she reached for the second envelope, blurring the return address. But even before she opened it, Rorie realized the letter was from Kate. Clay wouldn't write her, and everything Mary had wanted to say she'd already said the morning Rorie left Elk Run.

Three handwritten sheets slipped easily from the envelope, with Kate's evenly slanted signature at the bottom of the last.

The letter was filled with chatty news about Nightingale and some of the people Rorie had met. There were so many, and connecting names with the faces taxed her memory. Kate wrote about the county fair, telling Rorie that she'd missed a very exciting pig race. The biggest news of all was that after years of trying, Mary had finally won a blue ribbon for her apple pie— an honor long overdue in Kate's eyes.

Toward the end of the letter, Clay's fiancée casually mentioned that Clay would be in San Francisco the first week of September for a horse show. The American Saddlebreds from Elk Run were well-known throughout the Pacific coast for their fire and elegance. Clay had high hopes of repeating last year's wins in the Five Gaited and Fine Harness Championships.

Rorie's pulse shifted into overdrive and her fingers tightened on the letter. Clay was coming to San Francisco. He hadn't mentioned the show to Rorie—not once, although he must have known about it long before she'd left Nightingale.

Kate went on to say that she'd asked Clay if he planned to look up Rorie while he was in town, but he'd claimed there wouldn't be time. Kate was sure Rorie would understand and not take offense. She closed by mentioning that her father might also be attending the horse show and if he did, Kate would try to talk him into letting her tag along. Kate promised she'd phone Rorie the minute she arrived in town, if she could swing it with her father.

Not until Rorie folded the letter to return it to the envelope did she notice the postscript on the back of the last page. She turned over the sheet of pink stationery. The words seemed to jump off the page: Kate was planning an October wedding and would send Rorie an invitation. She ended with "Write soon."

Rorie's breath caught in her lungs. An October wedding... In only a few weeks; Kate would belong to Clay. Rorie closed her eyes as her heart squeezed into a knot of pain. It wasn't that she hadn't realized this was coming. Kate's and Clay's wedding was inevitable, but Rorie hadn't thought Clay would go through with it quite so soon. With trembling hands, she set the letter aside.

"RORIE, LOVE, I can't honestly believe you want to go to a horse show," Dan complained, scanning the entertainment section of the Friday-evening paper. They sat in the minuscule living room in her apartment and sipped their coffee while they tossed around ideas for something to do.

Rorie smiled blandly, praying Dan couldn't read her thoughts. He'd offered several suggestions for the night's amusement, but Rorie had rejected each one, until she pretended to hit upon the idea of attending the horse show.

"A horse show?" he repeated. "You never told me you were interested in horses."

"It would be fun, don't you think?"

"Not particularly."

"But, Dan, it's time to broaden our horizons—we might even learn something."

"Does this mean you're going to insist we attend a demolition derby next weekend?"

"Of course not. I read an article about this horse show and I just thought we'd enjoy the gaited classes and harness competitions. Apparently, lots of Saddlebreds and National Show Horses are going to be performing. Doesn't that interest you?"

"No."

Rorie shrugged, slowly releasing a sigh of regret. "Then a movie's fine," she said, not even trying to hide her disappointment. They'd seen each other only a handful of times since Rorie's return. Rorie wouldn't be going out with him tonight if he hadn't persisted. She hoped he'd soon get the message and start dating other women, but that didn't seem to be happening.

"I can't imagine why you'd want to see a horse show," Dan said once more.

For the past few days the newspapers had been filled with information regarding the country-wide show in which Kate had said several of Elk Run's horses would be participating. In all the years she'd lived in San Francisco, Rorie couldn't remember ever reading about a single equine exhibition, but then she hadn't exactly been looking for one, either.

If Dan refused to go with her, Rorie was determined to attend the event on her own. She didn't have any intention of seeking out Clay, but the opportunity to see him, even from a distance, was too tempting to let pass. It would probably be the last time she'd ever see him.

"I don't know what's gotten into you lately, Rorie," he complained, not for the first time. "Just when I think our lives are starting to even out, you throw me for a loop."

"I said a movie was fine." Her tone was testier than she meant it to be, but Dan had been harping on the same subject for weeks and she was tired of it.

If he didn't want her company, he should start dating someone else. She wasn't going to realize suddenly she was madly in love with him, as he seemed to expect. Again and again, Dan phoned to tell her that he loved her, that his love was enough for them both. She always stopped him there, unable to imagine spending the rest of her life with him. If she couldn't have Clay—and she couldn't—then she wasn't willing to settle for any-one else.

"I'm talking about a lot more than seeing a silly movie." He laid the newspaper aside and seemed to carefully consider his next words.

"Really, Dan, you're making a mountain out of a molehill," Rorie said. "Just because I wanted to do something a little out of the ordinary..."

"Eating at an Armenian restaurant is a little out of the ordinary," he muttered, frowning, "but horse shows... I can't even begin to imagine why on God's green earth you'd want to watch a bunch of animals running around in circles."

"Well, you keep insisting I've changed," she said flippantly. If she'd known Dan was going to react so strongly to her suggestion, she'd never have made it. "I guess this only goes to prove you're right."

"How much writing have you done in the past month?"

The question was completely unexpected. She answered him with a shrug, hoping he'd drop the subject, knowing he wouldn't.

"None, right? I've seen you sitting at your computer, staring into space with that sad look on your face. I remember how you used to talk about your stories. Your eyes would light up and sparkle. Enthusiasm would just spill out of you." His hand reached for hers, tightly squeezing her fingers. "What happened to you, Rorie? Where's the joy? Where's the energy?"

"You're imagining things," she said, nearly leaping to her feet in an effort to sidestep the issues he was raising. She reached for her purse and a light sweater, eager to escape the apartment, which suddenly felt too small. "Are you going to take me to that movie, or are you going to sit here and ask questions I have no intention of answering?"

Dan stood, smiling faintly. "I don't know what happened while you were on vacation, and it's not important that I do know, but whatever it was hurt you badly."

Rorie tried to deny it, but couldn't force the lie past her tongue. She swallowed and turned her head away, her eyes burning.

"You won't be able to keep pretending forever, Rorie. I know you too well. Put whatever it is behind you. If you want to talk about it, I've got a sympathetic ear and a sturdy shoulder. I'm your friend, you know."

"Dan, please..."

"I know you're not in love with me," he said gently. "I suspect you met someone else while you were away, but that doesn't matter to me. Whatever happened during those two weeks is over."

"Dan..."

He reached for her hand, pulling her back onto the sofa, then sitting down beside her. She couldn't look at him.

"Given time, you'll learn to love me," he cajoled, holding her hand, his voice filled with kindness. "We're already good friends, and that's a lot more than some people have when they marry." He raised her fingers to his mouth and kissed them lightly. "I'm not looking for passion. I had that with my first wife. I learned the hard way that desire is a poor foundation for a solid marriage."

"We've talked about this before," Rorie protested. "I can't marry you, Dan, not when I feel the way I do about...someone else." Her mouth trembled with the effort to suppress tears. Dan was right. As much as she hadn't wanted to face the truth, she'd been heartbroken from the moment she'd left Nightingale.

She'd tried to forget Clay, believing that was the best thing for them both, yet she cherished the memories, knowing those few brief days were all she would ever have of this man she loved.

"You don't have to decide right now," Dan assured her.

"There isn't anything to decide," she persisted.

His fingers continued to caress hers, and when he spoke his voice was thick. "At least you've admitted there is someone else."

"Was," she corrected.

"I take it there isn't any chance the two of you—"

"None," she blurted, unwilling to discuss anything that had to do with Clay.

"I know it's painful for you right now, but all I ask is that you seriously consider my proposal. My only wish is to take care of you and make you smile again. Help you forget."

His mouth sought hers, and though his kiss wasn't unpleasant, it generated no more excitement than before, no rush of adrenaline, no urgency. She hadn't minded Dan's kisses in the past, but until she met Clay, she hadn't known the warmth and magic a man's touch could create.

Dan must have read her thoughts, because he added in a soothing voice, "The passion will come in time— you shouldn't even look for it now, but it'll be there. Maybe not this month or the next, but you'll feel it eventually, I promise."

Rorie brushed the hair from her face, confused and uncertain. Clay was marrying Kate in just a few weeks. Her own life stretched before her, lonely and barren— surely she deserved some happiness, too. Beyond a doubt, Rorie knew Clay would want her to build a good life for herself. But if she married Dan, it would be an act of selfishness, and she feared she'd only end up hurting him.

"Think about it," Dan urged. "That's all I ask."

"Dan..."

"Just consider it. I know the score and I'm willing to take the risk, so you don't have to worry about me. I'm a big boy." He rubbed his thumb against the inside of her wrist. "Now, promise me you'll honestly think about us getting married."

Rorie nodded, although she already knew what her answer would have to be.

Dan heaved a sigh. "Now, are you really interested in that horse show, or are we going to see a movie?"

Rorie didn't need to think twice. "The movie." There was no use in tormenting herself with thoughts of Clay. He belonged to Kate in the same way that he belonged to the country. Rorie had no claim to either.

The film Dan chose was surprisingly good, a comedy, which was just what Rorie needed to lift her spirits. Afterward, they dined on linguine and drank wine and discussed politics. Dan went out of his way to be a pleasant companion, making no demands on her, and Rorie was grateful.

It was still relatively early when he drove her back to her apartment, and he eagerly accepted her invitation for coffee. As he eased the MG into the narrow space in front of her building, he suddenly paused frowning.

"Do you have new neighbors?"

"Not that I know of. Why?"

Dan nodded toward the battered blue pickup in the lot across the street. "Whoever drives that piece of junk is about to bring down the neighborhood property values."

CHAPTER FOURTEEN

"CLAY." His name escaped Rorie's lips on a rush of excitement. She jerked open the car door and stepped onto the sidewalk, legs trembling. Her pulse was thundering so hard it echoed in her ears like sonic booms.

"Rorie?" Dan called, agitated. "Who is this man?"

She hardly heard him. A door slammed in the distance and Rorie whirled around and saw that Clay had been siting inside his truck, apparently waiting for her return. He'd been parked in the shadows, and she hadn't noticed him there.

Dan joined her on the sidewalk and placed his hand possessively on her shoulder. His grip was the only thing that rooted her in reality, his hand the restraining force that prevented her from flying into Clay's arms.

"Who is this guy?" Dan asked a second time.

Rorie opened her mouth to explain and realized she couldn't, not in just a few words. "A...friend," she whispered, but that seemed so inadequate.

"He's a cowboy!" Dan hissed, making it sound as though Clay's close-fitting jeans and jacket were the garb of a man just released from jail.

Clay crossed the street and his long strides made short work of the distance separating him from Rorie.

"Hello, Rorie."

She heard the faint catch in his voice. "Clay."

A muscle moved in his cheek as he looked past her to Dan, who squared the shoulders of his Brooks Brothers suit. No one spoke for a long moment, until Rorie realized Clay was waiting for an introduction.

"Clay Franklin, this is Dan Rogers. Dan is the stockbroker I . . . I mentioned before. It was his sports car I was driving."

Clay nodded. "I remember now." His gaze slid away from Rorie to the man at her side.

Dan stepped around Rorie and accepted Clay's hand. She noticed that when Dan dropped his arm to his side, he flexed his fingers a couple of times, as though to restore the circulation. Rorie smiled to herself. Clay's handshake was the solid one of a man accustomed to working with his hands. When Dan shook hands, it was little more than a polite business greeting, an archaic but necessary exchange.

"Clay and his brother, Skip, were the family who helped me when the MG broke down," Rorie explained to Dan.

"Ah, yes, I remember you saying something about that now."

"I was just about to put on a pot of coffee," Rorie went on, unable to take her eyes off Clay. She drank in the sight of him, painfully noting the crow's feet that fanned out from the corners of his eyes. She couldn't remember them being quite so pronounced before.

"Yes, by all means join us." Dan's invitation lacked any real welcome.

Clay said nothing. He just stood there looking at her. Almost no emotion showed in his face, but she could feel the battle that raged inside him. He loved her still, and everything about him told her that.

"Please join us," she whispered.

Any lingering hope that Dan would take the hint and make his excuses faded as he slipped his arm protectively around Rorie's shoulders. "I picked up some Swiss mocha coffee beans earlier," he said, "and Rorie was going to brew a pot of that."

"Swiss mocha coffee?" Clay repeated, blinking quizzically.

"Decaffeinated, naturally," Dan hurried to add.

Clay arched his brow expressively, as if to say that made all the difference in the world.

With Dan glued to her side, Rorie reluctantly led the way into her building. "Have you been here long?" she asked Clay while they stood waiting for the elevator.

"About an hour."

"Oh, Clay..." Rorie felt terrible, although it wasn't her fault; she hadn't known he intended to stop by. Perhaps he hadn't known himself and had been lured to her apartment the same way she'd been contemplating the horse show.

"You should have phoned." Dan's comment was casual, but it contained a hint of accusation. "But then, I suppose, you folks tend to drop in on each other all the time. Things are more casual in the country, aren't they?"

Rorie sent Dan a furious glare. He returned her look blankly, as if to say he had no idea what could have angered her. Rorie was grateful that the elevator arrived just then.

Clay didn't comment on Dan's observation and the three stepped inside, facing the doors as they slowly closed.

"When you weren't home, I asked the neighbors if they knew where you'd gone," Clay mentioned.

"The neighbors?" Dan echoed, making no effort to disguise his astonishment.

"What did they tell you?" Rorie asked.

Clay smiled briefly, then sobered when he glanced at Dan. "They claimed they didn't know *who* lived next door, never mind where you'd gone."

"Frankly, I'm surprised they answered the door," Dan said conversationally. "There's a big difference between what goes on in small towns and big cities."

Dan spoke like a teacher to a grade-school pupil. Rorie wanted to kick him, but reacting in anger would only increase the embarrassment. She marveled at Clay's tolerance.

"Things are done differently here," Dan continued. "Few people have anything to do with their neighbors. People prefer to mind their own business. Getting involved can only lead to problems."

Clay rubbed the side of his face. "It seems to me *not* getting involved would lead to even bigger problems."

"I'm grateful Clay and Skip were there when *your* car broke down," Rorie said to Dan, hoping to put an end to this tiresome discussion. "Otherwise I don't know what would have happened. I could still be on that road waiting for someone to stop and help me," she said, forcing the joke.

"Yes," Dan admitted, clearing his throat. "I suppose I should thank you for assisting Rorie."

"I suppose I should accept your thanks," Clay returned.

"How's Mary?" Rorie asked, quickly changing the subject, as the elevator slid to a stop at her floor.

Humor sparked in Clay's gray eyes. "Mary's strutting around proud as a peacock ever since she won a blue ribbon at the county fair."

"She had reason to be proud." Rorie could just picture the housekeeper. Knowing Mary, she was probably wearing the ribbon pinned to her apron. "What about Skip?" Rorie asked next, hungry for news about each one. She took the keys from her purse and systematically began unlocking the three bolts on her apartment door.

"Fine. He started school last week—he's a senior this year."

Rorie already knew that, but she nodded.

"Kate wanted you to know she sends her best," Clay said next, his voice carefully nonchalant.

"Tell her I said hello, too."

"She hasn't heard from you. No one has."

"I know. I'm sorry. She wrote soon after I returned from Canada, but I hadn't had a chance to answer." On several occasions, Rorie had tried to force herself to sit down and write Kate a letter. But she couldn't. At the end of her second week back home, she'd decided it was better for everyone involved if she didn't keep in touch with Kate. When the wedding invitation came, Rorie planned to mail an appropriate gift, and that would be the end of it.

Once they were inside the apartment, Rorie hung up her sweater and purse and motioned for both men to sit down. "It'll only take a minute to put on the coffee."

"Do you need me to grind the beans?" Dan asked, obviously eager to assist her.

"No, I don't need any help." His offer was an excuse to question her about Clay, and Rorie wanted to avoid that if she could. At least for now.

Her apartment had never felt more cramped than it did when she joined the two men in her tiny living room. Clay rose to his feet as she entered, and the simple courtly gesture made her want to weep. He was telling her that he respected her and cared for her, that . . . she was his lady . . . would always be his lady.

The area was just large enough for one sofa and a coffee table. Her desk and computer stood against the other wall. Rorie pulled the chair away from the desk, turned it to face her guests and perched on the edge. Only then did Clay sit back down.

"So," Dan said with a heavy sigh. "Rorie never did tell me what it is you do in . . . in . . ."

"Nightingale," Rorie and Clay said together.

"Oh, yes, Nightingale," Dan murmured, clearing his throat. "I take it you're some kind of farmer? Do you grow soy beans or wheat?"

"Clay owns a stud farm for American Saddle-breds," Rorie explained.

Dan looked as if she'd punched him in the stomach. He'd obviously made the connection between Clay and her earlier interest in attending the horse show.

"I see," he breathed, and his voice shook a little. "Horses. So you're involved with horses."

Clay looked at him curiously.

"How's Nightsong?" Rorie asked, before Dan could say anything else. Just thinking about the foal with her wide curious eyes and her long wobbly legs produced a feeling of tenderness in Rorie.

"She's a rare beauty," Clay told her softly, "showing more promise every day."

Rorie longed to tell Clay how much it had meant to her that he'd registered Nightsong in her name, how she cherished that gesture more than anything in her life. She also knew that Clay would never sell the foal, but would keep and love her all her life.

An awkward silence followed, and in an effort to smooth matters over, she explained to Dan, "Clay was gone one night when Star Bright—one of the brood mares—went into labor...if that's what they call it in horses?" she asked Clay.

He nodded.

"Anyway, I couldn't wake up Skip, and I didn't know where Mary was sleeping and something had to be done—quick."

Dan leaned forward, his eyes revealing his surprise and shock. "You don't mean to tell me *you* delivered the foal?"

"Not exactly." Rorie wished now that she hadn't said anything to Dan about that night. No one could possibly understand what she and Clay had shared in those few hours. Trying to convey the experience to someone else only diminished its significance.

"I'll get the coffee," Rorie offered, standing. "I'm sure it's ready."

From her kitchen, she could hear Dan and Clay talking, although she couldn't make out their words. She filled three cups and placed them on a tray, then carried it into the living room.

Once more Clay stood. He took the tray out of her hands and set it on the coffee table. Rorie handed Dan the first cup and saucer and Clay the second. He looked uncomfortable as he accepted it.

"I'm sorry, Clay, you prefer a mug, don't you?" The cup seemed frail and tiny, impractical, cradled in his strong hand.

"It doesn't matter. If I'm going to be drinking Swiss mocha coffee, I might as well do it from a china cup." He smiled into her eyes, and Rorie couldn't help reciprocating.

"Eaten any seafood fettuccine lately?" she teased.

"Can't say that I have."

"It's my favorite dinner," Dan inserted, apparently feeling left out of the conversation. "We had linguine tonight, but Rorie's favorite is sushi."

Her eye caught Clay's and she noted how the corner of his mouth quirked with barely restrained humor. She could just imagine what the good people of Nightingale would think of a sushi bar. Skip would probably turn up his nose, insisting that the small pieces of raw fish looked like bait.

The coffee seemed to command everyone's attention for the next minute or so.

"I'm still reeling from the news of your adventures on this stud farm," Dan commented, laughing lightly. "You could have bowled me over with a feather when you announced that you'd helped deliver a foal. I would never have believed it of you, Rorie."

"I brought along a picture of Nightsong," Clay said, cautiously putting down his coffee cup. He unsnapped the pocket of his wide-yoked shirt and withdrew two color photographs, which he handed to Rorie. "I meant to show those to you earlier... but I got sidetracked."

"Oh, Clay," she breathed, studying the filly with her gleaming chestnut coat. "She's grown so much in just this last month," she said, her voice full of wonder.

"I thought you'd be impressed."

Reluctantly Rorie shared the pictures with Dan, who barely glanced at them before handing them back to Clay.

"Most men carry around pictures of their wife and kids," Dan stated, his eyes darting to Clay and then Rorie.

Rorie supposed this comment was Dan's less-than-subtle attempt to find out if Clay was married. Taking a deep breath, she explained. ''Clay's engaged to a neighbor—Kate Logan.''

"I see." Apparently he did, because he set aside his coffee cup, and got up to stand behind Rorie. Hands resting on her shoulders, he leaned forward and lightly brushed his mouth over her cheek. "Rorie and I have been talking about getting married ourselves, haven't we, darling?"

CHAPTER FIFTEEN

NO EMOTION revealed itself on Clay's face, but Rorie could sense the tight rein he held on himself. Dan's words had dismayed him.

"Is that true, Rorie?" he said after a moment.

Dan's fingers tightened almost painfully on her shoulders. "Just tonight we were talking about getting married. Tell him, darling."

Her eyes refused to leave Clay's. She *had* been talking to Dan about marriage, although she had no intention of accepting his offer. Dan knew where he stood, knew she was in love with another man. But nothing would be accomplished by telling Clay that she'd always love him, especially since he was marrying Kate within a few weeks. "Yes, Dan has proposed."

"I'm crazy about Rorie and have been for months," Dan announced, squarely facing his competition. He spoke for a few minutes more, outlining his goals. Within another ten years, he planned to be financially secure and hoped to retire.

"Dan's got a bright future," Rorie echoed.

"I see." Clay replaced his coffee cup on the tray, then glanced at his watch and rose to his feet. "I suppose I should head back to the Cow Palace."

"How...how are you doing in the show?" Rorie asked, distraught, not wanting him to leave. Kate would have him the rest of their lives; surely a few more minutes with him wouldn't matter. "Kate wrote that you were going after several championships."

"I'm doing exactly as I expected I would." The words were clipped, as though he were impatient to get away.

Rorie knew she couldn't keep him any longer. Clay's face was stern with purpose, drawn and resigned. "I'll see you out," she told him.

"I'll help you," Dan said.

She whirled around and glared at him. "No, you won't."

"Good to see you again, Rorie," Clay said, standing just inside her apartment, his hand on the door. His mouth was hard and flat and he held himself rigid, eyes avoiding hers. He stepped forward and shook Dan's hand.

"It was a pleasure," Dan said in a tone that conveyed exactly the opposite.

"Me, too." Clay dropped his hand.

"I'm glad you stopped by," Rorie told him quietly. "It was...nice seeing you." The words sounded inane, meaningless.

He nodded brusquely, opened the door and walked into the hallway.

"Clay," she said, following him out, her heart hammering so loudly it seemed to echo off the walls.

He stopped, and slowly turned around.

Now that she had his attention, Rorie didn't know what to say. "Listen, I'm sorry about the way Dan was acting."

He shook off her apology. "Don't worry about it."

Her fingers tightened on the doorknob, and she wondered if this was really to be the end. "Will I see you again?" she asked despite herself.

"I don't think so," he answered hoarsely. He looked past her as though he could see through the apartment door and into her living room where Dan was waiting. "Do you honestly love this guy?"

"He's . . . he's been a good friend."

Clay took two steps toward her, then stopped. As if it were against his better judgment, he raised his hand and lightly drew his finger down the side of her face. Rorie closed her eyes to the wealth of sensation the simple action provoked.

"Be happy, Rorie. That's all I want for you."

THE RAIN HIT during the last week of September, and the dreary dark afternoons suited Rorie's mood. Normally autumn was a productive time for her, but she remained tormented with what she felt sure was a terminal case of writer's block. She sat at her desk, her computer humming merrily as she read over the accumulation of an entire weekend's work.

One measly sentence.

There'd been a time when she could write four or five pages a night after coming home from the library. Perhaps the problem was the story she'd chosen. She wanted to write about a young filly named Nightsong, but every time she started, her memories of the real Nightsong invaded her thoughts, crippling the creative flow.

Here it was Monday night and she sat staring at the screen, convinced nothing she wrote had any merit. The only reason she even kept on trying was that Dan had pressured her into it. He seemed to believe her world would right itself once Rorie was back to originating her warm, lighthearted children's stories.

The phone rang and, grateful for a reprieve, Rorie hurried into the kitchen to answer it.

The unmistakable hum of a long-distance call echoed in her ear. "Is this Miss Rorie Campbell of San Francisco, California?"

"Yes, it is." Her heart tripped with anxiety. In a matter of two seconds, every horrible scenario of what could have happened to her parents or her brother darted through Rorie's mind.

"This is Devin Logan calling."

He paused, as though expecting her to recognize the name. Rorie didn't. "Yes?"

"Devin Logan," he repeated, "from the Nightingale, Oregon, Town Council." He paused. "I believe you're acquainted with my daughter, Kate."

"Yes, I remember Kate." If her heart continued at this pace Rorie thought she'd keel over in a dead faint. Just as her pulse had started to slow, it shot up again. "Has anything happened?"

"The council meeting adjourned about ten minutes ago. Are you referring to that?"

"No...no, I mean has anything happened to Kate?"

"Not that I'm aware of. Do you know something I don't?"

"I don't think so." This entire conversation was quickly driving her crazy.

Devin Logan cleared his throat, and when he spoke, his voice dropped to a deeper pitch. "I'm phoning on an official capacity," he said. "We voted at the Town Council meeting tonight to employ a full-time librarian."

He paused again, and not knowing what else to say, Rorie murmured, "Congratulations. Kate mentioned the library was currently being run by part-time volunteers."

"It was decided to offer *you* the position."

Rorie nearly dropped the receiver. "I beg your pardon?"

"My daughter managed to convince the council that we need a full-time librarian for our new building. She also persuaded us that you're the woman for the job."

"But..." Hardly able to believe what she was hearing, Rorie slumped against the kitchen wall, glad of its support. Logan's next remark was even more surprising.

"We'll match whatever the San Francisco library is paying you and throw in a house in town—rent-free."

"I..." Rorie's mind was buzzing. Kate obviously thought she was doing her a favor, when in fact being so close to Clay would be utter torment.

"Miss Campbell?"

"I'm honored," she said quickly, still reeling with astonishment, "truly honored, but I'm going to have to refuse."

A moment of silence followed. "All right...I'm authorized to enhance the offer by ten percent over the amount you're currently earning, but that's our final bid. You'd be making as much money as the fire chief, and he's not about to let the Council pay a librarian more than he's bringing home."

"Mr. Logan, please, the salary isn't the reason I'm turning down your generous offer. I...I want you to know how much I appreciate your offering me the job. Thank you, and thank Kate on my behalf, but I can't accept."

Another, longer silence vibrated across the wire, as though he couldn't believe what she was telling him.

"You're positive you want to refuse? Miss Campbell, we're being more than reasonable...more than generous."

"I realize that. In fact, I'm quite amazed and flattered by your proposal, but I can't possibly accept this position."

"Kate had the feeling you'd leap at the job."

"She was mistaken."

"I see. Well, then, it was good talking to you. I'm sorry we didn't get a chance to meet while you were in Nightingale. Perhaps next time."

"Perhaps." Only there wouldn't be a next time.

Rorie kept her hand on the telephone receiver long after she'd hung up. Her back was pressed against the kitchen wall, her eyes closed.

She'd regained a little of her composure when the doorbell chimed. A glance at the wall clock told her it was Dan, who'd promised to drop by that evening. She straightened forcing a smile, and slowly walked to the door.

Dan entered with a flourish, handing her a small white sack.

"What's this?" she asked.

"Frozen yogurt. Just the thing for a girl with a hot keyboard. How's the writing going?" He leaned forward to kiss her on the cheek.

Rorie walked back into the kitchen and set the container in the freezer compartment of her refrigerator. "It's not. If you don't mind, I'll eat this later."

"Rorie." Dan caught her by her shoulders and studied her face. "You're as pale as chalk. What's wrong?"

"I...I just got off the phone. I was offered another job as head librarian..."

"But, darling, that's wonderful."

"... in Nightingale, Oregon."

The change in Dan's expression was almost comical. "And? What did you tell them?"

"I refused."

He gave a great sigh of relief. His eyes glowed and he hugged her impulsively. "Does this mean what I think it does? Are you finally over that cowpoke, Rorie? Will you finally consent to be my wife?"

Rorie lowered her gaze. "Oh, Dan, don't you understand? I'll never get over Clay. Not next week, not next month, not next year." Her voice was filled with pain, and with conviction. Everyone seemed to assume that, given time, she'd forget all about Clay Franklin, but she wouldn't.

Dan's smile faded quickly, and he dropped his arms to his sides. "I see." He leaned against the counter, and after a long moment, he sighed pensively and said, "I'd do just about anything in this world for you, Rorie, but I think it's time we both faced a few truths."

Rorie had wanted to confront them long before now.

"You're never going to love me the way you do that horseman. We can't go on like this. It isn't doing either of us any good to pretend your feelings are going to change."

He looked so grim and so discouraged that she didn't point out that *he'd* been the one who'd been pretending.

"I'm so sorry to hurt you—it's the last thing I ever wanted to do," she told him sincerely.

"It isn't like I didn't know," he admitted. "You've been honest with me from the start. I can't be less with you. That country boy loves you. I knew it the minute he walked across the street without even noticing the traffic. The whole world would know," he admitted ruefully. "All he had to do is look at you and every-thing about him shouts his feelings. He may be en-gaged to another woman, but it's you he loves."

"I wouldn't fit into his world."

"But, Rorie, love, you're lost and confused in your own now."

She bit her lower lip and nodded. Until Dan said it, she hadn't realized how true that was. But it didn't change the fact that Clay belonged to Kate. And she was marrying him within the month.

"I'm sorry, Rorie," Dan said, completely serious, "but the wedding's off."

She nearly laughed out loud at Dan's announce-ment. No wedding had ever been planned. He'd asked her to marry him at least ten times since she'd returned from her vacation, and each time she'd refused. In-stead of wearing her down as he'd hoped, Dan had fi-nally come to accept her decision. Rorie felt relieved, but she was sorry to lose her friend.

"I didn't mean to lead you on," she offered, genu-inely contrite.

He shrugged. "The pain will only last a little while. I'm 'a keeper' as the girls in the office like to tell me. I guess it's time I let out the word that I'm available." He wiggled his eyebrows up and down, striving for some humor.

"You've been such a good friend."

He cupped her face and gently kissed her. "Yes, I know. Now don't let that yogurt go to waste—you're too thin as it is."

She smiled and nodded. When she let him out of the apartment, Rorie bolted the door then leaned against it, feeling drained, but curiously calm.

Dan had been gone only a short while when Rorie's phone rang again. She hurried into the kitchen to answer it.

The long-distance hum greeted her a second time. "Rorie? This is Kate Logan."

"Kate! How are you?"

"Rotten, but I didn't call to talk about me. I want to know exactly why you're refusing to be Nightingale's librarian—after everything I went through. I can't believe you, Rorie. How can you do this to Clay? Don't you love him?"

CHAPTER SIXTEEN

"KATE," RORIE DEMANDED. "What are you talking about?"

"You and Clay," she returned sharply, sounding quite unlike her normally gentle self. "Now, do you love him or not? I've got to know."

This day had been sliding steadily downhill from the moment Rorie had climbed out of bed that morning. To admit her feelings for Clay would only hurt Kate, and Rorie had tried so hard to avoid offending the other woman.

"Well?" Kate demanded, then gave a sob. "The least you can do is answer me."

"Oh, Kate," Rorie said, her heart in her throat, "why are you asking me if I love Clay? He belongs to you. It shouldn't matter one little bit if I love him or not. I'm out of your lives and I intend to stay out."

"But he loves you."

The tears in Kate's voice tore at Rorie's already battered heart. She would have given anything to spare her friend this pain. "I know," she whispered.

"Doesn't that mean anything to you?"

Only the world and everything in it. "Yes," she murmured, her voice growing stronger.

"Then how could you do this to him?"

"Do what?" Rorie didn't understand.

"Hurt him this way!"

"Kate," Rorie pleaded. "I don't know what you're talking about—I'd never intentionally hurt Clay. If you insist on knowing, I do love him, with all my heart, but he's your fiancé. You loved him long before I even knew him."

Kate's short laugh was riddle with sarcasm. "What is this? A game of first come, first served?"

"Of course not—"

"For your information, Clay isn't my fiancé any longer," Kate blurted, her voice trembling. "He hasn't been in weeks . . . since before he went to San Francisco for the horse show."

Rorie's head came up so fast she wondered whether she'd dislocated her neck. "He isn't?"

"That's . . . that's what I just got done telling you."

"But I thought . . . I assumed . . ."

"I know what you assumed—that much is obvious—but it isn't that way now and it hasn't been in a long time."

"But you love Clay," Rorie insisted, feeling almost light-headed.

"I've loved him from the time I was in pigtails. I love him enough to want to see him happy. Why . . . why do you think I talked my fool head off to a bunch of hard-nosed council members? Why do you think I ranted and raved about what a fantastic librarian you are? I as good as told them you're the only person who could possibly assume full responsibility for the new library. Do you honestly think I did all that for the fun of it? The challenge?"

"No, but, Kate, surely you understand why I have to refuse. I just couldn't bear to be—"

Kate wouldn't allow her to finish, and when she spoke, her voice was high and almost hysterical. "Well, if you think that, Rorie Campbell, then you've got a lot to learn about me…and even more to learn about Clay Franklin.''

"Kate, I'm sorry. Now, please stop and listen to me. There's so much I don't understand. We've got to talk, because I can't make heads or tails out of what you're telling me and I've got to know—"

"If you have anything to say to me, Rorie Campbell, then you can do it to my face. Now, I'm telling Dad and everyone else on the council that you've accepted the position we so generously offered you. The job starts in two weeks and you had damn well better be here. Understand?''

RORIE'S CAR LEFT a dusty trail on the long, curving driveway that led to the Circle L Ranch. It had been a week since her telephone conversation with Kate, and Rorie's mind still had trouble assimilating what the other woman had told her. Their conversation repeated itself over and over in her mind, until nothing made sense. But one thing stood out: Kate was no longer engaged to Clay.

Rorie was going to him, running as fast as she could, but first she had to settle matters with his former fiancée.

The sun had started to descend in an autumn sky when Rorie parked her car at the Logan ranch and climbed out. Rotating her neck and shoulders to relieve some of the tension coiled there, Rorie looked around, wondering if anyone was home. She'd been on the road most of the day, so she was exhausted. And exhilarated.

Luke Rivers strolled out of the barn, and stopped when he saw Rorie. His smile deepened. It could have been Rorie's imagination, but she sensed the hard edge was missing from his look, as though life had unexpectedly tossed him a good turn.

"So you're back," he said by way of greeting.

Rorie nodded, then reached inside the car for her purse. "Is Kate around?"

"She'll be here any minute. Kate's usually home from the school around four. Come inside and I'll get you a cup of coffee."

"Thanks." At the moment, coffee sounded like nectar from the gods.

Luke opened the kitchen door for her. "I understand you're going to be Nightingale's new librarian?" he said, following her into the house.

"Yes." But that wasn't the reason she'd come back, and they both knew it.

"Good." Luke brought down two mugs from the cupboard and filled them from a coffeepot that sat on the stove. He placed Rorie's cup on the table, then pulled out a chair for her.

"Thank you, Luke."

The sound of an approaching vehicle drew his attention. He parted the lace curtain at the kitchen window and glanced out.

"That's Kate now," he said, his gaze lingering on the driveway, softening perceptibly. "Listen, if I don't get a chance to talk to you later, I want you to know I'm glad you're here. I've got a few things to thank you for myself. If it hadn't been for you, I might have turned into a crotchety old saddle bum."

Before Rorie could ask him what he meant, he was gone.

Kate burst into the kitchen a minute later and hugged Rorie as though they were long-lost sisters. "I don't know when I've been more pleased to see anyone!"

Rorie's face must have revealed her surprise because Kate hurried to add, "I suppose you think I'm a crazy woman after the way I talked to you on the phone last week. I don't blame you, but...well, I was upset, to put it mildly, and my thinking was a little confused." She tossed her purse on the counter and reached inside the cupboard for a mug. She poured the coffee very slowly, as if she needed the time to gather her thoughts.

Rorie's mind was buzzing with questions she couldn't wait for Kate to answer. "Did I understand you correctly the other night? Did you tell me you and Clay are no longer engaged?"

Kate wasn't able to disguise the flash of pain that leaped into her deep blue eyes. She dropped her gaze and nodded. "We haven't been in weeks."

"But..."

Kate sat down across the table from Rorie and folded her hands around the mug. "The thing is, Rorie, I knew how you two felt about each other since the night of the Grange dance. A blind man would have known you and Clay had fallen in love, but it was so much easier for me to pretend otherwise." Her finger traced the rim of the mug. "I thought once you returned to San Francisco, everything would go back the way it was before you arrived."

"I was hoping for the same thing. Kate, you've got to believe me when I tell you I'd have done anything in the world to spare you this. When I learned you and Clay were engaged I wanted to—"

"Die," Kate finished for her. "I know exactly how you must have felt, because that's the way I felt later.

The night of the Grange dance, Clay kept looking at you. Every time you danced with a new partner, his frown grew darker. He might have had me at his side, but his eyes followed you all over the hall.''

"He loves you, too," Rorie told her. "That's what made this all so difficult."

"No, he doesn't," Kate answered flatly, without a hint of doubt. "I accepted that a long time before you ever arrived. Oh, he respects and likes me, and to Clay's way of thinking, that was enough." She hesitated, frowning. "To my way of thinking, it was enough, too. We probably would have married and found contentment over the years. But everything changed when Clay met you. You hit him square between the eyes, Rorie— a direct hit."

"I'm sure he feels more for you than admiration..."

"No," Kate said, reaching into her purse for a tissue. "He told me as much himself, but like I said, it wasn't something I didn't already know. You see, I was so crazy about Clay, I was willing to take whatever he offered me, even if it was only second-best." She swabbed at the tears that sprang so readily to her eyes and paused in an effort to gather her composure. "I'm sorry, Rorie. It's still so painful. But you see, through all this, I've leaned a great deal about what it means to love someone."

Rorie's own eyes welled with involuntary tears, which she hurriedly wiped aside. Then, Kate's fingers clasped hers and squeezed tight in a gesture of reassurance.

"I learned that loving people means placing their happiness before your own. That's the way you love Clay, and the same way he loves you." Kate squared her shoulders and inhaled a quavery breath.

"Kate, please, this isn't necessary."

"Yes, it is, because what I've got to say next is the hardest part. I need to ask your forgiveness for that terrible letter I wrote you soon after you left Nightingale. I don't have any excuse except that I was crazy with jealousy."

"Letter? You wrote me a terrible letter?" The only one Rorie had received was the chatty note that had told her about Mary's prize-winning ribbon and made mention of the upcoming wedding.

"I used a subtle form of viciousness," Kate replied her voice filled with self-contempt.

Rorie discounted the fact Kate could ever be malicious. "The only letter I received from you wasn't the least bit terrible."

Kate lowered her eyes to her hands, neatly folded on the table. Her grip tightened until Rorie was sure her friend's long nails would cut her palms.

"I lied in that letter," Kate continued. "When I told you that Clay wouldn't have time for you while he was at the horse show, I was trying to tell you that you didn't mean anything to him anymore. I wanted you to think you'd easily slipped from his mind when nothing could have been further from the truth."

"Don't feel so bad about it. I'm not sure I wouldn't have done the same thing."

"No, Rorie, you wouldn't have. That letter was an underhand attempt to hold on to Clay... I was losing him more and more each day and I thought... I hoped that if you believed we were going to be married in October, then... Oh, I don't know, my thinking was so warped and desperate."

"Your emotions were running high at the time." Rorie's had been, too—she understood Kate's pain because she'd been in so much pain herself.

"But I was pretending to be your friend when in reality I think I almost hated you." Kate paused, her shoulders shaking with emotion. "That was the crazy part. I couldn't help liking you and wanting to be your friend, and at the same time I was being eaten alive with selfish resentment."

"It's not in you to hate anyone, Kate Logan."

"I . . . I didn't think it was, either, but I was wrong. I can be a terrible person, Rorie. Facing up to that hasn't been easy."

"Then...a few days after I mailed that letter to you, Clay came over to the house wanting to talk. Almost immediately I realized I'd lost him. Nothing I could say or do would change the way he felt about you. I said some awful things to Clay that night . . . He's forgiven me now, but I need your forgiveness, too."

"Oh, Kate, of course, but it isn't necessary. I understand. I honestly do."

"Thank you," she murmured, blotting her eyes with the crumpled tissue. "Now I've got that off my chest, I feel a whole lot better."

"But if Clay had broken your engagement when he came to San Francisco, why didn't he say anything to me?"

Kate shrugged. "I don't know what happened while he was gone, but he hasn't been himself since. He never has been a talkative person, but he seemed to draw even further into himself when he came back from seeing you. He's working himself into an early grave, everyone says. Mary's concerned about him—we all are.

Mary said if you didn't come soon, she was going after you herself.''

''Mary said that?'' The housekeeper had been the very person who'd convinced Rorie she was doing the right thing by getting out of Clay's life.

''Well, are you going to him? Or are you determined to stick around here and listen to me blubber all day? If you give me any more time,'' she said, forcing a laugh, ''I'll manage to make an even bigger fool of myself than I already have.'' Kate stood abruptly, pushing back the kitchen chair. Her arms were folded around her waist, her eyes bright with tears.

''Kate,'' Rorie murmured, ''you are a dear, dear friend. I owe you more than it's possible to repay.''

''The only thing you owe me is one godchild—and about fifty years of happiness with Clay Franklin. Now get out of here before I start weeping in earnest.''

Kate opened the kitchen door for her and Rorie gave her an impulsive hug before hurrying out.

Luke Rivers was standing in the yard, apparently waiting for her. When she came out of the house he sauntered over to her car and held open the driver's door. ''Did everything go all right with Kate?''

Rorie nodded.

''Well,'' he said soberly, ''There may be more rough water ahead for her. She doesn't know it yet, but I'm buying out the Circle L.'' Then he smiled, his eyes crinkling. ''She's going to be fine, though. I'll make sure of that personally.'' He extended his hand, gripping hers in a firm handshake. ''Let me be the first to welcome you to our community.''

''Thank you.''

He touched the rim of his hat in farewell, then glanced toward the house. "I think I'll go inside and see how Kate's doing."

Rorie's gaze skipped from the foreman to the house and then back again. "You do that." If Luke Rivers had anything to say about it, Kate wouldn't be suffering from a broken heart for long. Rorie had suspected Luke was in love with Kate. But like her, he was caught in a trap, unable to reveal his feelings. Perhaps now Kate's eyes would be opened—Rorie fervently hoped so.

The drive from the Logans' place to the Franklins' took no more than a few minutes. Rorie parked her car behind the house, her heart pounding like a piston in a hot engine. When she climbed out, the only one there to greet her was Mary.

"It's about time you got here," the housekeeper complained, marching down the porch steps with a vengeance.

"Could this be the apple-pie blue-ribbon holder of Nightingale, Oregon?"

Mary actually blushed, and Rorie laughed. "I thought you'd never want to see the likes of me again," she teased.

"Fiddlesticks." The weathered face broke into a smile.

"I'm still a city girl," Rorie warned.

"That's fine 'cause you got the heart of one from the country." Wiping her hands dry on her apron, Mary reached for Rorie and hugged her.

After one brief, bone-crushing squeeze, she set her free. "I'm a meddling old woman and I suspect the good Lord intends to teach me more than one lesson in the next year or two. I'd best tell you that I never should have said those things I did about Kate being the right woman for Clay."

"Mary, you spoke out of concern. I know that."

"Clay doesn't love Kate," she continued undaunted, "but my heavens, he does love you. That boy's been pining his heart out for want of you. He hasn't been the same from the minute you drove out of here all those weeks ago."

Rorie had suffered, too, but she didn't mention that to Mary. Instead, she slipped her arm around the housekeeper's broad waist and together they strolled toward the house.

"Clay's gone for the day, but he'll be back within the hour."

"An hour," Rorie repeated. She'd waited all this time; another sixty minutes shouldn't matter.

"It'll be dinnertime then, and it's not like Clay or Skip to miss a meal. Dinner's been the same time every night since I've been cooking for this family, and that's a good many years now." Mary's mouth formed a lopsided grin. "Now what we'll do is this. You be in the dining room waiting for him and I'll tell him he's got company."

"But won't he notice my car?" Rorie twisted around gesturing at her old white Toyota—her own car this time—parked within plain sight.

Mary shook her head. "I doubt it. He's never seen your car, so far as I know, only that fancy sports car. Anyway, that boy's been working himself so hard, he'll be too tired to notice much of anything."

Mary opened the back door and Rorie stepped inside the kitchen. As she did, the house seemed to fold its arms around her in welcome. She paused, and breathing in the scent of roast beef and homemade biscuits. It might not be sourdough and Golden Gate Park rose blossoms, but it felt right. More than right.

"Do you need me to do anything?" Rorie asked.

Mary frowned then nodded. "There's only one thing I want you to do—make Clay happy."

"Oh, Mary, I intend to start doing that the minute he walks through that door."

An hour later, almost to the minute, Rorie heard Skip and Clay come into the kitchen.

"What's for dinner?" Skip asked immediately.

"It's on the table. Now wash your hands."

Rorie heard the teenager grumble as he headed down the hallway to the bathroom.

"How'd the trip go?" Mary asked Clay next.

He mumbled something Rorie couldn't hear.

"The new librarian stopped by to say hello. Old man Logan and Kate sent her over—thought you might like to meet her."

"I don't. I hope you got rid of her. I'm in no mood for company."

"Nope," Mary said flatly. "Fact is, I invited her to stay for dinner. The least you can do is wipe that frown off your face and go introduce yourself."

Rorie stood just inside the dining room, her heart ready to explode. By the time Clay stepped into the room, tears had blurred her vision and she could hardly make out the tall, familiar figure that blocked the doorway.

She heard his swift intake of breath, and the next thing she knew, she was crushed in Clay's loving arms.

CHAPTER SEVENTEEN

RORIE WAS LOCKED so securely in Clay's arms that for a moment she couldn't draw a breath. But that didn't matter. What mattered was that she was being hugged by the man she loved and he was holding on to her as though he didn't plan to ever let her go.

Clay kissed her again and again, the way a starving man takes his first bites of food, hesitant at first, then eager. The palms of Rorie's hands were pressed against his chest and she felt the quick surge of his heart. His own hand was gentle on her hair, caressing it, running his fingers through it.

"Rorie . . . Rorie, I don't believe you're here."

Rorie felt the power of his emotions, and they were strong enough to rock her, body and soul. This man really did love her. He was honest and hardworking, she knew all that, but even more, Clay Franklin was *good*, with an unselfishness and a loyalty that had touched her deeply. In an age of ambitious, hardhearted, vain men, she had inadvertently stumbled on this rare man of character. Her life would never be the same again.

Clay exhaled a deep sigh, and his hands framed her face as he dragged his head back to gaze into her eyes. The lines that marked his face seemed more deeply incised now, and she felt another pang of sorrow for the pain he'd endured.

"Mary wasn't teasing me, was she? You are the new librarian?"

Rorie nodded, smiling up at him, her happiness shining from her eyes. "There's no going back for me. I've moved out of my apartment, packed everything I own and quit my job with little more than a few days' notice."

Rorie had fallen in love with Clay, caught in the magic of one special night when a foal had been born. But her feelings stretched far beyond the events of a single evening and the few short days they'd spent together. Her love for Clay had become an essential part of her. Rorie adored him and would feel that way for as long as her heart continued to beat.

Clay's frown deepened and his features tightened briefly. "What about Dan? I thought you were going to marry him."

"I couldn't," she said, then smiled tenderly, tracing his face with her hands, loving the feel of him beneath her fingertips.

"But—"

"Clay," she interrupted, "why didn't you tell me that night in San Francisco you'd broken your engagement to Kate?" Her eyes clouded with anguish at the memory, at the anxiety they'd caused each other. It had been such senseless heartache, and they'd wasted precious time. "Couldn't you see how miserable I was?"

A grimace of pain moved across his features. "All I noticed was how right you and that stockbroker looked together. You both kept telling me what a bright future he had. I couldn't begin to offer you the things he could. And if that weren't enough, it was all too apparent that Dan was in love with you." Gently Clay smoothed her hair away from her temple. "I could understand what it meant to love you, and between the two of us, he seemed the better man."

Rorie lowered her face, pressing her forehead against the hollow of his shoulder. She groaned in frustration. "How can you even think such a thing, when I love you so much?"

Clay moved her face so that he could gaze into her eyes. "But, Rorie . . ." He stopped and a muscle jerked in his jaw. "Dan can give you far more than I'll ever be able to. He's got connections, background, education. A few years down the road, he's going to be very wealthy—success is written all over him. He may have his faults, but basically he's a fine man."

"He *is* a good person and he's probably going to make some woman a good husband. But it won't be me."

"He could give you the kinds of things I may never be able to afford. . . ."

"Clay Franklin, do you love me or not?"

Clay exhaled slowly, watching her. "You know the answer to that."

"Then stop arguing with me. I don't love Dan Rogers. I love you."

Still his frown persisted. "You belong in the city."

"I belong with you," she countered.

He said nothing for a long moment. "I can't argue with that," he whispered, his voice husky with emotion. "You do belong here, because God help me, I haven't got the strength to let you walk away a second time."

Clay kissed her again, his mouth sliding over hers as though he still couldn't believe she was in his arms. She held on to him with all her strength, soaking up his love. She was at home in his arms. It was where she belonged and where she planned to stay.

The sound of someone entering the room filtered through to Rorie's consciousness, but she couldn't bring herself to move out of Clay's arms.

"Rorie," Skip cried, his voice high and excited, "what are you doing here?"

Rorie finally released Clay and turned toward the teenager who had come to her rescue that August afternoon.

"Hello, Skip," she said softly. Clay slipped his arm around her waist and she smiled up at him, needing his touch to anchor her in the reality of their love.

"Are you back for good?" Skip wanted to know.

She nodded, but before she could answer, Clay said, "Meet Nightingale's new librarian." His arm tightened around her.

The smile that lit up the teenager's eyes was telling. "So you're going to stick around this time." He blew out a gusty sigh. "It's a damn good thing, because my brother's been as hard to live with as a rattlesnake since you left."

"I'd say that was a bit of an exaggeration," Clay muttered, clearly not approving of his brother's choice of descriptions.

"You shouldn't have gone," Skip said, sighing again. "Especially before the County Fair."

Rorie laughed. "You're never going to forgive me for missing that, are you?"

"You should have been here, Rorie. It was great."

"I'll be here next summer," she promised.

"The fact is, Rorie's going to be around a lifetime of summers," Clay informed his brother. "We're going to be married as soon as it can be arranged." His eyes held hers but they were filled with questions, as if he half expected her, even now, to refuse him.

Rorie swallowed the emotion that bobbed so readily to the surface and nodded wildly, telling him with one look that she'd marry him any time he wanted.

Skip folded his arms over his chest, and he gave them a smug look. "I knew something was going on between the two of you. Every time I was around you guys it was like getting zapped with one of those stun guns."

"We were that conspicuous?" It still troubled Rorie that Kate had known, especially since both she and Clay had tried so hard to hide their feelings.

Skip's shrug was carefree. "I don't think so, but I'm not much into love and all that nonsense."

"Give it time, little brother," Clay murmured, "because when it hits, it'll knock you for a loop."

Mary stepped into the room, carrying a platter of meat. "So the two of you are getting hitched?"

Their laughter signaled a welcome release from all the tensions of the past weeks. Clay pulled out Rorie's chair, then sat down beside her. His hand reached for hers, lacing their fingers together. "Yes," he said, still smiling, "we'll be married as soon as we can get the license and talk to the pastor."

Mary pushed the basket of biscuits closer to Skip. "Well, you don't need to fret—I'll stick around for a couple more years until I can teach this child the proper way to feed a man. She may be pretty to look at, but she don't know beans about whipping up a decent meal."

"I'd appreciate that, Mary," Rorie said. "I could do with a few cooking lessons."

The housekeeper's smile broadened. "Now, go ahead and eat before the potatoes get cold and the gravy gets lumpy."

Skip didn't need any further inducement. He reached for the biscuits, piling three on the edge of his plate.

Mary reached down and playfully slapped his hand. "I've got apple pie for dessert, so don't go filling your-selves up on my buttermilk biscuits." Her good humor was evident as she surveyed the table, glancing at every one's plate, then bustled back to the kitchen.

Rorie did her best to sample a little of everything. Although the meal was delicious, she was too excited to do anything as mundane as eat.

After dinner, Skip made himself scarce. Mary deliv-ered a tray with two coffee cups to the living room, where Clay and Rorie sat close together on the couch. "You two have lots to talk about, so you might as well drink this while you're doing it."

"Thank you, Mary," Clay said, sharing a smile with Rorie.

The older woman set the tray down, then patted the fine gray hair at the sides of her head. "I want you to know how pleased I am for you both. Have you set the date yet?"

"We're talking about that now," Clay answered. "We're going to call Rorie's family in Arizona this eve-ning and discuss it with them."

Mary nodded. "She's not the woman I would have chosen for you, her being a city girl and all, but she'll make you happy."

Clay's hand reached for Rorie's. "I know."

"She's got a generous soul." The housekeeper looked at Rorie and her gaze softened. "Fill this house with children—and with love. It's been quiet far too long."

The phone rang in the kitchen and with a regretful glance over her shoulder, the housekeeper hurried to answer it. A moment later, she stuck her head around the kitchen door.

"It's for you, Clay. Long distance."

Clay's grimace was apologetic. "I'd better answer it."

"You don't need to worry that I'll leave," Rorie teased. "You're stuck with me for a lot of years, Clay Franklin."

He kissed her before he stood up, then headed toward the kitchen. Rorie sighed and leaned back, cradling her mug in both hands. By chance, her gaze fell on the photograph of Clay's parents, which rested on top of the piano. Once more, Rorie felt the pull of his mother's eyes. She smiled now, understanding so many things. The day she'd planned to leave Elk Run, this same photograph had captured her attention. The moment she'd walked into this house, Rorie had belonged to Clay, and somehow, looking at his mother's picture, she'd sensed that, from the farthest corner's of her heart. She belonged to this home and this family.

Clay returned a few minutes later, with old Blue following him. "Just a call from the owner of one of the horses I board. Just checking on his prize," he said, as he sat down beside Rorie and placed his arm around her shoulder. His eyes followed hers to the photo. "Mom would have liked you."

Rorie sipped her coffee and smiled. "I know I would have loved her." Setting her cup aside, she reached up and threw both arms around Clay's neck. Gazing into his eyes, she brought his mouth down to hers.

Perhaps it was her imagination, or an optical illusion—in fact, Rorie was sure of it. But she could have sworn the elegant woman in the photograph smiled.

*Kate Logan falls in love again, and Luke Rivers
achieves his fondest dreams in
Debbie Macomber's COUNTRY BRIDE
(Harlequin Romance #3059).
Available in June
wherever paperback books are sold.*

HARLEQUIN
Romance®

Coming Next Month

#3043 MOUNTAIN LOVESONG Katherine Arthur
Lauren desperately needs help at her northern California holiday lodge, so when John Smith, handyman *extraordinaire*, appears out of nowhere, he seems the answer to her prayers. The only question—how long can she depend on him?

#3044 SWEET ILLUSION Angela Carson
Dr. Luke Challoner, arrogant and domineering, expects everyone to bow to his will. He is also one of the most attractive men Marion has ever met—which doesn't stop her from standing up for herself against him!

#3045 HEART OF THE SUN Bethany Campbell
Kimberly came home to Eureka Springs to nurse a broken heart. Alec Shaughnessy came to examine Ozark myth and folklore. Both become entangled in a web of mystery that threatens to confirm an old prophesy—that the women in Kimberly's family might never love happily.

#3046 THAT CERTAIN YEARNING Claudia Jameson
Diane's heart goes out to vulnerable young Kirsty, but warning bells sound when she meets Kirsty's dynamic and outspoken uncle, Nik Channing. Yet she has to support Kirsty, even if it means facing up to her feelings... and to Nik.

#3047 FULLY INVOLVED Rebecca Winters
Fight fire with fire—that was how Gina Lindsay planned to win back her ex-husband. Captain Grady Simpson's career as a firefighter had destroyed his marriage to Gina three years earlier. But now she's returned to Salt Lake City—a firefighter, too....

#3048 A SONG IN THE WILDERNESS Lee Stafford
Amber is horrified when noted journalist Lucas Tremayne becomes writer-in-residence at the university where she is secretary to the dean. For Luke had played an overwhelming part in her teenage past—one that Amber prefers stay hidden....

Available in April wherever paperback books are sold, or through Harlequin Reader Service:

In the U.S.
901 Fuhrmann Blvd.
P.O. Box 1397
Buffalo, N.Y. 14240-1397

In Canada
P.O. Box 603
Fort Erie, Ontario
L2A 5X3

This April, don't miss Harlequin's new Award of Excellence title from

Harlequin Presents...

CAROLE MORTIMER

Award of Excellence

---

elusive as the unicorn

When Eve Eden discovered that Adam Gardener, successful art entrepreneur, was searching for the legendary English artist, The Unicorn, she nervously shied away. The Unicorn's true identity hit too close to home....

Besides, Eve was rattled by Adam's mesmerizing presence, especially in the light of the ridiculous coincidence of their names— and his determination to take advantage of it! But Eve was already engaged to marry her longtime friend, Paul.

Yet Eve found herself troubled by the different choices Adam and Paul presented. If only the answer to her dilemma didn't keep eluding her....